Conflict of Interests

A Novel by William Tyler Horn

Conflict of Interests

A Novel by William Tyler Horn

Printed by Lulu.com

ISBN #978-0-6151-6361-1

I don't know who first described Los Angeles as a gorgeous yet unpredictable woman, but I think they were right. LA is breathtaking to look at, she is exciting to be in, too damned expensive, and she just might hurt you at any minute. Still I love this city like an abused husband.

My friends call me Jordan. I'm a recently divorced 37-year-old comic looking for an honest relationship in Los Angeles. I know what you're thinking; good luck in a town best known for its silicone breasts and Hollywood B.S. I only dream of meeting a woman who I will love as much as I do my newfound freedom? If couples did allow more independence in their marriages divorce lawyers would be in the unemployment line right behind the most of the actors, writers, and comedians in Hollywood.

Excuse me I have to get up and call yet another woman who would rather do her hair than talk to me. I got her voice mail and didn't want to come off sounding like a stalker so I hung up. LA is a city that thrives on cash, good looks, and connections. Hell I would have settled for just one out of three, because I'm a comic. All I want is a woman with just low enough self-esteem to be attracted to me. It's such a comfort to have these fantasies coupled with a sense of humor. Most women claim they want a man who can make them laugh. That could be true, but not in bed. I'm convinced the only reason most women in Los Angeles ever engage in sex is to achieve that aerobic burn.

What intrigues me is when a woman is needy, there are boatloads of guys willing to sacrifice their egos marching through her emotional mine field to marry her. When a man is equally as desperate, women flee in the opposite direction like you are The Elephant Man with Tourette's Syndrome.

A perfect example is my roommate and best friend Peggy. She is a 38-year-old, 6-foot, 200-pound blond with a temper like Hitler just after he'd quit crack cocaine. Yet men vie for her attention like a dog under a glass dinner table begging for scraps. Could it possibly be the fact that her breasts rival the peaks of Mount Everest? No. Men are not that shallow. Sure we are and we admit it. Face it for a man to flirt as successfully as a woman in Los Angeles he'd have to wear his wallet outside of his pants.

Why didn't I fall for Peggy? It was not for lack of effort. We have lived together for five years, but mostly as friends. Our few forays into sex were so uneventful that our bedroom could have been renamed Death Valley. After our fumbling attempts at lovemaking we would look at each other like a couple attending a truly bad film, wondering why we had shown up at all. However, this has never intruded on one of the best friendships either of us ever had, and being roommates was never dull.

Observing Peggy date was both awkward and amusing at the same time. Witnessing my attempts at dating were merely painful. I observed an endless stream of men pursue Peggy with Herculean vigor, gifts, and worst manners than at a WWF Smack Down.

One of her first stud boys was a real estate agent named Dale, who wined and dined Peggy. He swore that all he wanted was an exclusive relationship. The last time they went out Dale was looking so hard at other women that she almost needed his head restrained in a neck brace. Dale called Peggy three times in a row to cancel a date at the last minute from his car phone. The last time he called to cancel on his cell phone Peggy actually overheard him having oral sex while he was talking with her. Yet this didn't even temper the termination her troublesome trysts.

Her next decadent dude was a Mid Eastern construction worker named Hussein. He plied Peggy with lots of lingerie, fine food, pot, and during sex he wore a bright red genital-ring. I told her that using a prop during sex was like an athlete using steroids. Peggy insisted that whatever it took to cross the sexual finish line was okay with her. I thanked her for sharing. Once she called Hussein and a strange female answered the phone. He swore up and down it was his sister who had come over to clean his apartment, and Peggy believed him. At this point I stopped watching "Sex In The City," because Peg's love life was far more interesting than Sara Jessica Parker's. I was relieved that at least one of us had a social life. Hell if it weren't for the Playboy channel I wouldn't have had a sex life at all.

Sure there was nothing but a lot of squiggly lines on my TV, because I was too cheap to pay the $6.95. But, I knew there was a breast in there somewhere.

On the other hand Peggy was humping Hussein in every conceivable location, except when his sister was over cleaning his apartment. Once they even were doing the wild thing in the elevator of Peggy's apartment building when the door opened to a surprised Dale. He had arrived with flowers and an apology. Peggy graciously accepted the flowers, and then the elevator door slammed shut. To his credit Hussein didn't even miss a stroke.

This was even more bizarre than the relationship I had with my ex wife. I couldn't believe it when my ex left me for another woman. Now I had to pay alimony to both of them. Isn't paying alimony like buying gas for a stolen car? I knew something was up when my ex screamed out the name of her gynecologist during sex, and her OBGYN was a female. I understood that I might have to make changes to make my marriage work. I just didn't think my ex wanted me to be a woman too. Later I discovered that the OBGYN was seeing at my wife nude more often than I was.

Almost out of pity Peggy kept pushing me into dates. My first inauspicious liaison was with a woman named Katherine. She critiqued the restaurant, the meal, my pathetic little car, and then me. It was like dating Roger Ebert in a dress.

Too many women think men only have one thing on their minds. Not true. I was thinking is Katherine going to chip in for that steak and lobster too?

I'll admit that the waiter was churlish and the steak was blood red. I was surprised that when it hit her plate, it didn't make a break for the door.

Katherine "The Great" then proceeded to accuse me of everything except the Holocaust, Watergate, and the O.J. mishaps. By the way, the O.J. murders, that was me. After reaming me in her car I asked her, "Does this mean the wedding is off?" She slammed the car door so hard I almost lost a finger. I guess Katherine failed to grasp the healing powers of humor. I guess she reminded me of my ex wife. My ex was an emotional terrorist who took no prisoners. Once I begged her to talk dirty to me. Her answer was, "Kiss my ass." She said if I had really cared about her I would have married someone else.

It was hard to decide which was more painful, my divorce or the actual marriage. I can't believe that some people compare divorce to a prison release. No way. When you get out of jail they give you $200 dollars and a new suite of clothes. Next time I get serious about a woman I am going to be sure she is worth the alimony first.

Somewhere out there I'm certain there are married people having great sex, just not in my bedroom. Before we could have sex she wanted the yard work done, the garage cleaned, and to go shopping with her. Was this some secret form of foreplay I was not aware of? Men could never get away with holding out for sex to get what we want, because sex is what we want. This is why women are in charge. Look at what most women's priorities are; financial security, companionship, children, and hopefully true love. These are intelligent objectives. What do men want? How about sex that doesn't cost a $100 an hour, and an occasional ballgame? That could be why there are tons of magazines for brides, but grooms have none. O.K.: men do have Playboy, Penthouse, Big Butt Biker Babes, and Swank.

9

It is no great mystery that when a woman walks down the aisle she is generally ecstatic where men are terrified. To get married men are willing to give up their freedom, their car, their house, half of their income, and all of their opinions. What do women give up? I don't know what? Their jobs?

I digress, but only to illustrate why Peggy wanted to run headlong towards the altar while I cautiously backed away from it. All of the above comments aside I love women. You have to, because the alternatives are so darned ugly.

I just want a woman to be an equal partner not an eternal need machine. My friends keep telling me to read these relationship "Mars and Venus" self help books. Most of these books don't tell you on how to get along with women. They try to turn you into one.
I think I already tried that and it didn't work.
It was entirely my fault for wanting to do something productive or fun with my wife. Instead my ex wanted me to listen for endless hours to unsolvable problems. I am willing to lend an ear for an hour or

so, but not until five in the morning unless there is some hot monkey love involved.

The next woman I met was a gorgeous beach blonde. She was a statuesque 5'10", and her name was Noella. After a few steamy dates we had fallen completely in lust with one another. The sex was so intense I thought it was love. I should have been suspicious when Noella first told me she supported herself with her art. Later I found out that Art was a wealthy Hollywood TV producer. It also turned out that Art was terminally married. I discovered this when I accidentally over heard Art propositioning Noella, while I was holding on the other phone line.

Noella and I met later that evening. I mentioned that I had overheard Art offering her money for sex. I also asked what else she was not telling me. A tearful Noella then regaled me with her clichéd tale of woe. She had arrived in LA, a young girl from a small mid-western town, and tried to make it in Hollywood. Unfortunately she did this by making it with half of Hollywood as a high priced call girl.

I always wondered how Noella could afford that beachfront condo on an artist's salary. Again I proved to myself that love is not only blind, but is deaf, dumb, and stupid as well.

Idiot that I am I told her I loved her anyway. Noella told me she wanted to get married but she couldn't trust me to be faithful, because I worked in nightclubs. She couldn't trust me? Isn't that like your lawyer demanding that you tell **him** the truth? I could have asked Noella to quit her business, but she might have told me to do the same. Irony is such a cruel mistress and so was Noella.

We were still in lust when she began her vacation on a Mediterranean cruise, and I left on a four-week stand-up tour in the not so Deep South.

I had a disquieting feeling when we parted, and not just because of where I was headed. Noella was vacationing with the beautiful people. Where I was going I would be lucky to run into someone with a full set of teeth, and an IQ larger than their hat size.

However, inbreeding should not be sold short. Look what it's done for England's Royal family.

When I arrived in Alabama I was so far out in the country all I could hear were dogs baying at the moon, and that was inside the nightclub. You really know your jokes are bombing when all you can hear from the stage is a farm boy choking his chicken. And I do mean his bird. I met everyone in town named Buford, Cletus, Festus, and Goober, and those were the women. My audiences looked chillingly like rejects from a monster truck rally.

I couldn't get enough of that New Orleans blackened food and somebody named Billy Bob asking me if it was spicy enough for me. Spicy enough? I felt like my colon was on fire and smoke was billowing out of my pants. It was enough to make me long for LA police beatings, earthquakes, brush fires, riots, and occasional gunfire. I didn't drive out of the Deep South I fled to the airport.

Right after we landed at LAX through that comforting brown blanket of smog I called Noella.

13

I suppose I was a sucker for pain. I was not to be disappointed. It seemed while I had been gone for four weeks Noella saw fit to marry a wealthy Australian rancher she had met on her cruise. If I had any pride I wouldn't have been crushed. Instead, when got home I wept like a hormonal high school girl. This same night I was booked to do a show at the best Comedy Club in Hollywood for some big time movie producers. I couldn't eat or sleep. Peggy was comforting, until her beau-of-the-month showed up. Then she whipped out the door with a box of chocolates and a head full of marriage plans. Peggy made Gandhi look like a pessimist.

There I sat in a candle lit bath sobbing on the phone with an apologetic Noella. He excuse was that I probably wasn't going to marry her anyway. I asked if that meant she had the right to begin deceiving yet another man. In her eyes sure it did. I asked if she were going to quit LA and move to Australia, and would her "Johns" accept this intercontinental arrangement?

Once again the healing powers of humor were elusive, but this time for both of us.

One thing Noella taught me was if you're on a date and a woman asks, "You're not a cop are you?" It is wise do a background check on her immediately.

When I finally arrived at The Comedy Club I was a disheveled mess. My best comic buddy Travis straightened me up, and then told me some funny filthy jokes. Yet the clouds of despair deepened. Travis warned me that these big time producers were booking writers and actors for a film project, and I could not afford to blow this one off. I thanked him for pointing out the obvious, and then trudged sullenly toward the backstage area. My name was seventh on a list of about twenty-five comics.

It was a prime slot, but I could not have been more depressed. The comic on stage was killing, and the other acts were begging me for my time slot.

The guy performing just before me went on to a tepid burst of apathy, and struggled to get any response at all. Thanks for the dynamite lead in pal.

The bombing comic finally rapped up his angst filled set. Then the emcee desperately tried to resuscitate the audience with some comedic CPR. Suddenly my name and credits were being announced, and a shock of adrenaline shot through out my entire body. When I reached the microphone I froze for a second and then something magical happened. I can't quite explain how the cloud lifted. I got my first laugh and then proceeded to rock the entire room with laughter. The industry guys were rolling in the isles. I felt warm undulating waves of audience adulation wafting over me. Sensational sex with someone you adore couldn't have been any more exhilarating. The crowd was having a laughter orgasm and I was their comedy stud muffin. At that moment I knew I had ascended into comedy nirvana.

I exited the stage to an ecstatic embrace of affection and congratulations from everyone. Then I spotted Peggy and her date trying to push through the crowd. I smiled and waved. Several industry guys were blowing enough smoke up my ass to start a Malibu brush fire. I wish Noella had been here to witness all this. When I told Peggy that she insisted it was her loss, because I was going to be a huge star. It didn't matter to me, because I couldn't share this with anyone I was in love with. There was joy all around me yet I felt completely alone. Peggy and Travis tried to cheer me up, but it was to no avail.

Slowly my focus shifted from my friends to the radiant smile of this fair skinned red head. It was like she was walking towards me in slow motion.

I could scarcely believe it. This stunning woman was about to speak to me, and all I could do was smile awkwardly. She told me her name was Erin McNamara. I said, "It seems a little touch of Irish heaven has floated here to earth." Erin beamed and told me how much she had enjoyed my act.

I joked, "I respect your lack of taste Erin." When she laughed I knew I was hooked. I couldn't believe I was once more willing to approach the altar of love. I didn't care. I figured if you are not willing to take a chance on loosing your heart you are the only one who will ever own it.

Then two producers named Bob and Harvey walked up to us. They wanted to turn my stand up act into a TV film. One even asked if Erin and I were married. My face turned redder than her hair. She laughed and put her hand in my rear butt pocket. The only reason my ex wife ever reached into my pants was to get a better grip on my wallet.

With Erin's hand on my left ass cheek it was difficult to admit to Bob and Harvey that we had just met. I certainly could not let on that she and I would rather to be alone. All I did was thank Bob and Harvey for their interest in me. Then I whisked Erin away before I made a complete fool of myself.

I scarcely knew this vision in red and already I was willing to ignore my career just to be alone with her, and she knew it. However Erin was considerate enough to ask, "Shouldn't you stay and talk to those guys? They seemed really interested your act."

I explained, "I'm much too curious about you. Besides they know where to find me."

When we excused ourselves and exited the club. Erin revealed, "I'm glad I came by myself tonight. I can't ever remember meeting someone who was good looking and funny." I responded by walking right into a parking meter on the way to her car. She laughed. "You did that on purpose didn't you?"

I admitted, "I don't have to fake being goofy. It comes quite naturally." Erin moved closer to me.

She kissed me deeply. "Does this come naturally too?"

I could barely answer, "Lord I hope so." Our embrace was so long and passionate I almost forgot where I was.

Suddenly Peggy and her beau appeared. "Please don't stop on our account Jordan," Peggy commented. "Shouldn't you two take that indoors? I wondered where you two had gone."

It was difficult making introductions with a mouthful of Erin. So I mumbled, "Peggy this is Erin. Erin this is Peggy and her friend, uh...."

Peggy interjected, “This is my friend Ron, but I'm sure you two want to get back to what you were doing. So we'll talk later, bye." Then they left.

Erin said, “I think we had better get in my car." I nodded in agreement as we entered the plush tan leather interior of her teal blue Mercedes.

I blurted out, "Please don't tell me you're an artist."

Erin responded. "No I am a lawyer. This is a lease car. My boss wants me to drive it to impress our clients."

"Thank God they never expect you to maintain a false facade in show business." She chuckled. I looked directly into her bright blue eyes. "Finally someone who appreciates my sense of humor."

Erin returned my serene gaze and breathed, "That's not all I appreciate about you Jordan." Our lips met, our tongues entwined, and our bodies tingled with the excitement of what was to come. We paused just long enough to drive to Erin's house.

When we entered her house my heart was pounding so rapidly I though we would have to call the love paramedics. Whatever despair I had felt earlier in the evening was a distant memory by now. Life's vicissitudes never cease to amaze me. My head was now filled with a thousand questions. Most of them were rooted in my insecurities, but if I didn't open my mouth she might never know. Was I being dishonest? Hell no I was being intelligent. Something men rarely are, especially around beautiful women. I was just wondering how quickly we should proceed when Erin dimmed the lights, and put on a delicate Mozart sonata. Well I guess there wasn't going to be a lot of small talk. She led me over to an overstuffed antique couch. I tried to speak, but her full lips quickly covered mine. Her hands roamed feverishly over my yielding body. I couldn't believe that fate had sent me this magnificent female and she actually seemed to like me. Before long our discarded garments traced a trail into Erin's bedroom.

Were we moving too quickly? Of course we were. Did either of us care? Not for a nano-second.

Making love to Erin was like floating effortlessly in a warm azure sea of pure pleasure, where all thoughts revolved around taking us both to even greater heights of ecstasy.

Erin moaned, "I never want this night to end."

I couldn't believe it when I assured her. "It never has to."

Erin queried, "Do you really mean that?"

I smiled and replied, "I've never been so sure of anything in my life."

Erin looked perplexed. "We know so little about one another."

"We sure could have a lot of fun finding out." She grinned and nodded her head yes as our bodies spooned perfectly into one another. I had just pledged myself to this incredible woman, and was completely comfortable with it. It was hard to believe that there was no alcohol involved. OK Perhaps there was a little.

Without any warning my mind began to race. Am I nuts? Wasn't I the same bitterly divorced guy who teased Peggy about running headlong towards commitment without a care in the world? Now I was about to do the same thing and on the first night. Which led me to ask, "Do you think we should slow things down a little?"

"Isn't it a little too late for that?" She grinned knowingly.

I had to admit, "I guess you're right, but now comes the hard part."

"You mean trying to talk to a man after making love before he has a chance to fall asleep on you?" Erin hugged me good-naturedly.

"We do that don't we? I'm afraid if drop off you might leave. Maybe I'll wake up and discover this has all been an incredible dream. I can't ever admit this to my friend Peggy. I just rushed into something I told her not to do."

"You mean sleeping with someone you just met?" Erin asked.

"Nope. Sleeping with a lawyer." I joked.

Meanwhile, back at Peggy's, she and her new boyfriend were busy discussing Erin and me. Peggy opined, "Ron that is exactly the type of women Jordan told me was his Achilles heel. He warned if she were Irish had red hair and he was a prisoner of love."

"Come on she was so pale you could practically see through her." Ron insisted.

"Ron, she was drop dead gorgeous."

"Not if you ever have to go outdoors. .1 prefer my women a lot healthier looking," Ron assured Peggy.

"Boy I am thankful for that."

"Do you think they are talking about us right now Peggy?"

"It didn't look to me like there was going to be a whole lot of talking going on," Peggy observed.

At Erin's, conversation was exactly what was happening. Long ago I realized how naive young men are. They think relationships are about sex. Hey you have to stop and talk some time, and the older you get the more talking it takes.

Erin and I lay there, bathed in the luminescent afterglow of our lovemaking. What could I say next so that my newfound love would never want me to leave? I mumbled, "Does any of your family live here locally?"

This was the best I could come up with? Then something totally unexpected happened next. Out of nowhere tears began flowing down Erin's cheeks.

I held her snugly and kissed her on the forehead. "Was I that bad?" I asked, attempting some humor.

"No of course not." She grinned tearfully. "We were fantastic together. It's just been so long since I've allowed myself to feel this vulnerable around anyone. After my really rocky childhood and what I've been through with men lately, I thought I would never feel this way again. I am sorry Jordan. I didn't mean to put you off."

"Erin you never have to apologize to me for your feelings."

Erin dried her eyes. "I guess it was the way I was raised. I think my father must have wanted a boy. He always told me to stop blubbering or I'll give you something to cry about."

"I can't believe it. That's exactly what my father used to say. Did dads everywhere consult this universal cliché hand book on how to whip their kids into shape?"

"I hope your father didn't follow it up with a fist or a belt?"

I hugged Erin so lovingly that she knew the answer was yes. I tried consoling her. "Don't worry Erin no one is ever going to hurt you again. Not while I'm around."

Erin kissed me full on the lips, with tears streaming down her face. Then she asked, "Do you really mean that, Jordan?"

"More than anything."

Erin kissed me on the cheek then on the lips. Both out faces were moist with tears of hope. She felt so incredible in my arms that I was dying to say

I love you, but was too afraid of the awkward pause that might follow.

Erin filled the potential silence with, "I know what you are thinking."

"What would that be?"

"That you are hungry? What would you like to eat?"

My anticipation was replaced with a knowing chuckle. "Oh yeah food. Whatever you've got would be fine."

Back at Peggy's, Ron's sleaziness had begun to surface. The more he pressed his move the more Peggy insisted, "Ron, I know there's a mutual attraction here, but I am very serious about commitment."

"But we just met," Ron pleaded.

"All the more reason to get to know one another better before things get too serious."

"I guess that mean no sex tonight huh?" Ron inquired indelicately.

That next morning at Erin's I suddenly realized my pitiful little car was parked back at The Comedy

Club. How could get Erin to drop me off without her spotting me climbing into my embarrassment-mobile? Before I could craft a strategy Erin asked, "I guess you need a ride to your car?"

"You can just drop me at the club. I don't remember quite where I parked." I hedged.

Erin kissed me. "Last night was so steamy it erased your entire memory? Boy I am good. Let's get going."

As we headed out the front door, we noticed another vehicle blocking her car in the driveway. Slowly this huge side of beef in black leather ominously slithered out of his customized Cadillac. Erin became noticeably agitated.

She eyed him with an icy composure. "Earl I told you a long time ago we were through, and never wanted to see you again. Leave right now and I won't call the police." She whipped out her cell phone.

Earl moved very quickly for a big gorilla. In one swift motion he snatched the cell phone out of Erin's hand and crushed it under his huge foot.

He sneered menacingly. "Looks like this damn thing is broke in half, Erin. Just like that little shit is gonna be." Earl shot me a stare that stone froze my blood.

Suddenly I remembered my promise to protect Erin, but not from Godzilla in cow hide. Then I wondered what would Clint Eastwood do. First off Clint would have a .44 magnum the most powerful handgun in the world. I didn't. Second Clint was 6'4" and had a nasty sneer. I was a goofy looking 5'9" in heels. Earl lumbered closer and looked directly into my eyes. I was so petrified I couldn't even blink. I knew that if Earl got even a whiff of my fear I would be kissing the pavement. Earl snarled, "I'm going to yank out your heart and dance to the beat, boy."

I couldn't believe my answer. "Very colorful, Earl, but it's not going to happen. Not now; not ever."

Earl seemed surprised. "Why the hell not?"

"Because, you look a little young to die."

Earl was stunned that I was standing up to him. To tell you the truth so was I. Earl countered with, "Die? Hell, I just wanted to kick your ass."

I realized my next words would be critical. So I snarled, "I don't fight. I kill people. So get your ass out of here now while you're still breathing." Earl's eyes widened considerably as I nervously stuck my hand inside my open jacket.

I was in disbelief. It was as if I had channeled Clint. Then an even more amazing thing happened. The bewildered Earl grimaced, stalked to his car, and drove off without a word. Right after I'd caught my breath Erin ran over and hugged me. She enthused, "Jordan, you are the first man who has ever risked his life for me. That is so sweet." Then we scrambled into her car before Earl decided to come back. Erin was still astounded at seeing a side she didn't know I had. Hell I didn't even know I had it. "Where did this tough guy act come from?" She inquired.

I confessed, "It came from Clint Eastwood. In "Outlaw Josie Wales" he backed down a bounty hunter that way. So I figured it might work on Earl."

Erin kissed me. "You learned that from Clint? I can't wait to see what else he taught you. You were magnificent." I thought me magnificent? No I was just lucky for the third time in recent memory. I figured if she was going for it, why confuse her.
Erin was late for work so she dropped me off right in front of The Comedy Club. I waited until she was well out of sight to sneak off to my poor car. My ride was so lame. I may as well have owned a Gremlin with an eight-track. It didn't matter. I drove off with a silly grin on my face and a song in my heart.

Once I was at Peggy's, we compared notes on our dates minus certain specifics. She could not believe Ron had exited so quickly once the subject of commitment was brought up. I suggested, "Perhaps introducing the subject of commitment on the first date was a little premature Peggy."

Peggy responded defiantly, "How else was I going to know how serious Ron was about us? It wasn't like I opened up a bridal magazine and asked him to pick out a wedding dress."

For the first time I had a successful date and Peggy didn't. I was usually the one who needed a shoulder to cry on. I knew I had to display a sensitivity that men, especially comedians, rarely have. I pointed out, "Didn't you want to find out if this guy was the real deal first Peggy?"

She ardently insisted, "I am 38 years old and I don't have any more time to waste. What I have been doing so far hasn't worked so why not try something else?"

I was immediately contrite. "I apologize, Peg. I made the mistake of thinking like a man again. I've got to remember to stop doing that. Fortunately I didn't do that last night." Did you ever want to be able to stuff words back in your mouth? Maybe she didn't catch my slip up.

Peggy detected that I had unwittingly revealed more than I'd wanted to. She pried. "Exactly what did you do last night? When we left you two at the car I'll bet you fell for her. You did didn't you? I can tell you did by that goofy grin on your face."

I was so incredibly busted. If I had pleaded the 5th and she found out later I was in major trouble. So lying was out of the question, or was it? I stammered, "Well sure we hit it off."

Peggy smiled. "The red hair was real wasn't it?"

I couldn't believe I had begun to blush. Between the stammering and the blushing I must have resembled as 15-year old school boy. Peggy knew I was in love and there was no hiding it. I had hoped to tell Erin first but I'm sure she already knew.

Peggy would not let up. "Come on Jordan. This time I had a miserable date and you didn't. I have a right to know what happened. You owe me."

I capitulated. "You know she is my type. Yes I really like her and I am pretty sure of sure she feels the same way."

Peggy was unrelenting. "I don't want the Disney version. I want details. The juicier the better."

There was no way I could call off this inquisition. So I divulged, "I didn't tell her I loved her if that's what you are getting at. I did promise to protect her and then had to prove it the next morning."

"I was sure when you didn't come home last night you were falling for her. I knew it."

"All right, last night was incredible. You were there for the beginning of it. Right now I am lucky to be here with all my requisite body parts intact."

"She was that good, huh?" Peggy joked.

"Yes she was, thank you. Unfortunately, her ex-boyfriend was not too thrilled this morning when he caught us leaving her place."

Knowing my reluctance when it comes to violence, Peggy was beside herself with curiosity. "What did you do, joke your way out of it, Jordan? You don't fight."

I told her how channeling Clint Eastwood had saved two lives that morning, and allowed me to make good on my promise to protect Erin. Peggy admitted that an act of heroism, especially from an insecure short guy like me, would have really impressed her. She asked when I was going to see Erin again and to keep her posted. I insisted that it made me feel like a sleazy tabloid reporter. In view of the fact that I was now the one with the love life, I guess it was my turn. Subsequently, Peggy remembered that Erin had called. I realized I would immediately have to explain to Erin that Peggy and I were only roommates. At Erin's that evening she asked, "Who was the woman who answered the phone at your place? Should I be jealous?"

"Peggy and I are just friends. I assured her. You met her with her date last night. Remember when we were kissing in front of your car?"

Erin tilted her head back and laughed. "Oh that really big woman with the little guy. That's right. She said she would see you later. I was paying a lot more attention to you at the time, Jordan." When she hugged me both of us were relieved.

I sniffed her hair. "You smell terrific. What is that perfume?"

"It is flea dip shampoo." Erin giggled.

"That is a turn on. You didn't tell me you had this problem."

"I don't my dog Eli does. At least now the house is free of ticks and fleas. You want to meet him."

Then I felt something moist on my ankle, and it was licking its way up my leg. "I think I already have." Right before Eli could get any closer to my crotch Erin admonished him.

"Stop it Eli. He is mine."

I shook my head. "Just my luck. I fall for the one red-head in Hollywood who owns a gay dog."

"Eli is not gay he's sensitive. That is his way of getting to know you better."

"I'm just happy if he doesn't bite me or hump my leg. Most dogs feel compelled to."

Erin snuggled and looked imploringly into my eyes, and then we kissed. "Can we get to bed early? I have to catch a plane first thing in the morning."

When I remembered how Noel had dumped me right after a road trip I froze for a moment. Erin sensed my uneasiness. She inquired, “What's wrong? It's only a deposition I have to take in Seattle. I'm going to be back in a couple of days. Oh you are going to miss me. That is so sweet."

I tried my best not to let my phobia regarding failed loves get in the way. But, there was that abandonment specter of Noel perched on my psyche, right along side of my ex-wife. Hadn't I dealt with these issues enough in therapy? Erin thought my reaction was cute. So I let it slide. I reminded myself: *don't blow the love of a lifetime and smoldering leaving town sex over something stupid.* Cool was something I rarely was, except tonight. The thought of making love to Erin was just too overpowering. Her very touch made me quiver with anticipation. So help me even the odor of that flea shampoo was making me hotter than a Santa Ana breeze. As we slipped out of our clothes and into the bedroom, I silently prayed that Erin would still want to see me when she got back to Los Angeles.

I returned to The Comedy Club the following evening, mostly out of the frustration of not being able to be with Erin. I discovered that doing stand up and hanging out with other comics was not exactly a substitute for being with someone you are falling in love with. A couple of comics pestered me about those film producers Bob and Harvey. I told them I had been too busy to call them yet. All Travis wanted to know about was that fabulous red head.

I've played comedy clubs for over twelve years and this was the first time I could ever remember feeling like a popular guy. One thought invariably haunts me when things are going well. Something bad has to happen just to keep you from getting too cocky. That dark cloud no sooner drifted through my brain when in the door walked the very same movie producers who had seen me the night I met Erin. I hope they aren't pissed.

Both of them came right over to me. Before I could apologize Bob asked, "We wondered what had happened to you Jordan. Did you have an out of town gig or something?" I was certain the next words I'd be hearing would be that they had given the movie project to someone else.

I was about to answer but Bob interjected, "Every comedian and writer in this town has been busting our balls to get on board with this film project. We didn't hear a word from you. So we decided that kind of indifference could only mean one thing. This has to be our guy."

All I could do was shake their hands in agreement then said, "Well thank you. Thank you so much."

Bob turned to Harvey and said, "See already he's funny." Harvey nodded in agreement. Bob added, "Are you doing a show here tonight, or do you want to go somewhere else and talk about our project?"

My immediate reaction was to think that I must have been dreaming. However, the odor of Bob's after-shave was so strong I knew I couldn't be. I suggested, "Let's go somewhere else and talk about the project." I wasn't quite quick enough, because just then the MC walked over and told me I was performing in a two minutes. Was this the first shoe dropping? You see comedy is a lot like sports. You always plan to play your best game, but way deep down you know that any night you could stink up the joint. I thought what the heck it was just a career.

Then I heard the MC announce, "Let's give it up for the comedy of Jordan Tyler ladies and gentlemen." I rushed onto the stage with absolutely no idea of what I was about to say, but I opened my mouth and began anyway. "I know what you are thinking. Nice clothes. I'll bet this guy never throws anything out. You're right. And, I'm divorced, depressed, and beginning to look way too much like my dad. Soon I'll start wearing high water pants up to my man boobs, the butt will slide south, and I'll start chasing kids out of my yard with a rake. White guys get to a certain age and they loose their butts. It's a Caucasian thing. Get to fifty. It's gone. Seventy and it's inverted. I asked my dad what happened to his butt. He yelled, "I worked my ass off for you, young man!" They were buying so I continued. "I was married for four and a half years. I got six months off for good behavior. My ex wife told me she wanted to make a difference in my life. She did. I'm dating men now. Sure I used to be heterosexual, before I got married."

I asked, "Why can't women come with an instructional manual? My ex said she faked orgasms. Why? Because, she had to. She told me she closed her eyes during sex, so she could pretend she was shopping. Men fantasize about having two women at the same time. Married men always have two women. The woman you married and the one she turns into every 28 days. You know the difference between a woman on PMS and a terrorist? You can negotiate with a terrorist. Women have two men too. The man she married and the one she tries to turn him into. Why do men want two women in bed? Easy. That way you can disappoint **more** than one woman at a time? That's what we do best isn't guys? Disappoint."

I smiled. "Love means having to say you're sorry every five damn minutes. Guys should start every day like this. Sweetheart everything is entirely my fault, and I'll never ever do it again. Then buy her flowers and jewelry, because men know they can't get through one whole day without screwing up somehow. Remember, women are always right and they don't play fair. I know. I used to be a woman. (Laughter) Look at a woman's advantages. If a man takes his clothes off in public, he gets locked up with a lot of butt ugly criminals. If a woman strips in public she gets a $600,000 K advance from Playboy. If a male teacher sleeps with a female student he is branded a pervert. If a female teacher has sex with a male student he is the luckiest bastard who ever lived. I know, because I was that student. Now if a man talks dirty to a woman, and she gets pissed, it's sexual harassment."

"If a woman talks dirty to a man it can cost you $3.95 a minute. Unless the prices have gone up."

Then I glanced over and saw that the industry guys loved it. I had fooled them again. So I said, "Thank you so much and good night." Then I bailed.

The first one who ran over to me was Travis, because Bob and Harvey were in deep conversation. I thought perhaps congratulations were in order, but all Travis wanted to talk about was my fabulous redhead. I attempted to escape backstage, but Travis was on me like pit bull on a postal worker. He started right in. "I know you are trying to hide something from your old buddy Travis. You know how I know? I shook my head no. Travis contended, "If this red head had been high maintenance or one of them LA wallet vampires you'd be doing jokes on her right now; but you're not. She had to be a hottie or you wouldn't have that shit eating' grin on your face."

Travis continued his harangue. "Come on man lay it on me. I'm dateless and desperate damn it."

"Don't pull a Helen Keller on now me Jordan. I'll bet you think I want to move on her don't you?" I looked at Travis unsmilingly. "Look Travis I don't mind if you borrow jokes or money from me now and again, because you are a friend. I don't even care if you go to the bathroom right before the check arrives at a restaurant, so I get stuck for the tab. However, I will never tell you anything about the fabulous redhead. I have never been a very possessive person, but this woman is **all mine.** Got it?"

Travis was stunned into a stony silence for a minute. Then he hesitantly answered, "Sorry. I didn't know you were all that serious about her."

Now I felt like I had to apologize. "Look I know you are a really nice guy Travis. You don't act like it sometimes, but you are." Fortunately he took all this in stride.

Neither of us knew that movie producer Bob had been listening at the backstage door the entire time. He was smirking from ear to ear. Bob announced, "That was perfect. Between Jordan's monologue on men and women and this type of banter, it's exactly what we want in this project. It's a guy talk verses girl talk type of thing."

I tried to hard to assure him. "Wait Bob we can write a quality script if you really want. It can be a lot more intelligent than what you've seen here."

Bob joked, "Intelligent? Please Jordan its television. We have to keep it basic. After all we are shooting for a 20 something demographic on this thing. Just like the politician said, keep it simple stupid. Hell maybe I said that."

Travis chimed in. "I got no problem with stupid Bob."

Bob admonished, "I was talking to Jordan."

I jumped in to try to save Travis's ego. "He was speaking euphemistically Bob. Right Travis?"

Travis shrugged. "Sure whatever the heck euphemistically means."

Bob smiled and said, "See that is exactly the kind of dumb I'm looking for."

Travis grinned moronically and shrugged.

Bob smiled benignly. "Come on guys lets get out of here and talk some serious show business."

"I'm ready Bob. You can't say no to a decent paying job in comedy?" When we started for the door I couldn't help noticing the hangdog look on Travis's face. It made me feel so guilty I had to ask, "Can Travis come with us Bob? We write together?"

Bob tried to be nice. "I don't have the say so to hire your friend Travis, but if you write with him I guess he can come along. Harvey is waiting outside in the car. Let's move it."

As we exited the club looks of envy radiated from the other comics like heat waves wafting off a searing summer sidewalk. I should have known right then that no one at The Comedy Club would ever view us the same way again. Maybe this won't be such a bad thing.

Bob and Harvey took us to a very up scale restaurant in Hollywood called Spagos. Compared to other patrons Travis and I looked like a couple of homeless guys. Bob and Harvey marched right in and sat down like they owned the place.

Travis and I looked at one another, shrugged, and followed them to a corner booth. We all enjoyed a very productive development meeting on the direction of the script. For the first time in ages I felt really good about my life and myself. When in the door walks Erin with a fantastic looking guy in a three-piece designer suit. I tried to ignore the obvious, which was difficult, because Travis kept elbowing me in the ribs. Fortunately Bob and Harvey didn't notice.

Even with Erin seated out of our view, Travis was even more distracted than I was. He could not wait to ask the myriad of questions exploding in his brain. I shot him a stern look so we could continue our meeting. I was relieved when we had finally left Spagos. At least Travis waited for Bob and Harvey to take us to his van before he began hurling questions at me.

Travis started right in. "O.K. Jordan who was that rich dude with your red head? Why didn't she tell you she was back in town? You got to be really pissed about this. Aren't you?"

I tried my best to remain composed. "I don't know any more than you do Travis. She may have tried to call. I was at the club with you remember? I am not going to make any assumptions before I talk with her." At least that's what I told him. Inside I was being overwhelmed by the uncertainties running rampantly through out my brain. The suspense of not knowing was killing me. So I quickly excused myself, got in my looser mobile, and headed directly for Erin's place.

When I got to Erin's house I parked out of view, so she wouldn't think I was checking up on her. I had never snooped on anyone before. This was so embarrassing, but the alternative of a Noella type of emotional ambush was even more ominous. Erin's car pulled up soon after I had arrived. I was relieved to discover no one else was with her. Now my dilemma was to find out who she had been with, without Erin thinking I was spying on her.

So I went to a near by pay phone and called her number. She was excited that I had called, and wanted me to come right over. I was so relieved, because that phone booth was getting mighty chilly.

When Erin opened the door she looked so breath taking that all of the silly questions about the mystery man at Spagos immediately flitted out of my brain. The luminous lights of Los Angeles paled in comparison to her incandescent smile. This woman could make the gray skies bluer. She could make it rain whenever she wanted to. She could make a castle out of a single grain of sand, and she could make a ship sail on dry land. Oh yes she can. The Temptations always said it better than I ever could.

"Didn't you get my message saying I'd returned early and that missed you?"

I immediate thought, from the looks of that sucker in the three piece you sure couldn't have missed me that much. Fortunately it only remained a thought. She went on to explain, "I was called back to LA early for an emergency meeting with an in town client. My boss tried to get him together with another lawyer in our firm, but he wanted me."

"Yeah I'll bet he did."

Erin grinned mischievously. "If I didn't know any better I'd say you were jealous. It's all right. I think it's cute."

I was dying to know more about this sharp dressed man, but when Erin practiced her feminine wiles on me, all of my unresolved insecurities about her blissfully drifted away. This was a woman who clearly understood all of her feminine powers. I was completely aware of the spell Erin was weaving and yet I loved succumbing to it. The way she would gently touch me and simultaneously show a hint of cleavage would drive my passion beyond all reason.

I ruminated. Is there ever any clear thinking going on when you are falling in love? Not really. Again I wondered how could I be letting my guard down so soon after being dumped by Noella, and trashed by my ex wife?

Why do I ask myself these inane questions on the way to a bedroom full of unbridled ecstasy? I vowed to shut my brain off unless Erin yelled out another guy's name while we were making love. Actually it would be a lot more embarrassing if I yelled out another guy's name during the act.

I returned home the next morning and couldn't even get through breakfast before Peggy called. She always seemed to call when I was eating. I answered the phone with a mouthful of muffin, "Hi who is it?"

"I caught you eating again didn't I? Good then I can ask all the questions. This is the second night you haven't come home, and you haven't even hinted you are in love yet. Well are you, and when are you going to bring her over?"

I swallowed hard. "At what point did you become my mother? She didn't even grill about my love life as much as you do. Couldn't this wait until you get home from work?"

Peggy whispered, "It is going to have to. I think I hear my boss coming. Talk at you later. Bye."

I hung up and dove back into my food in the hope of finishing it before the phone rang again. I was not quite quick enough. This time it was Travis. Neither of us could believe we were up before the crack of noon. He was even more persistent than Peggy. "Can't you see this Erin is just a rebound thing Jordan. Noella just crushed your onions and you turn around and hop on red. What's up with that?"

This was one of those times you were praying for your call waiting to beep. I countered. "Travis all relationships are on the rebound unless you're a virgin. It is only a matter of the timing. I told you how I felt about Erin. So back the hell off."

"I'm sorry. I was just trying to save you some grief buddy."

My prayer was answered when my call waiting beeped. So I cut off Travis's diatribe with, "Someone's on the other line Travis. Got to go. Beep. Hello. Peggy? No I haven't finished eating yet. Let me go. The other line is beeping. Beep. Who is this? Bob? Oh thank God."

Bob acknowledged, "You are a hard man to find. When I called last night a woman answered the phone, and I don't think it was your red head. Did she tell you that we wanted a meeting with you today? The studio is anxious to get this project off the ground. Is that your other line beeping?"

I answered anxiously, "Damn Bob I'm sorry. It's been a little frantic this morning. Please don't go anywhere I'll be right back." I beeped in call waiting and impatiently demanded, "Who is this? Peggy? I can't talk now. No it's not Erin. It's Bob about the film. Why the hell didn't you tell me he called? It's a lot more important than my love life. I'm sorry I hung up on you. Got to go. Bye." I beeped Bob back in and apologized. "I'm really sorry Bob. No it was not important. Your call is. Where and when do you want to meet? Lunch this afternoon? Sure. No. Travis can't make it. I'll see you there in an hour. Bye."

Upon leaving my place I couldn't help wondering if Erin's sucker in the three-piece suit was actually a professional acquaintance. Then my mind shifted to Peggy's fascination with my love life. Was it because, she lacked one? Then I wondered if Travis was jealous of Erin for the same reason? Then the car behind me leaned on his . He was probably one of those West LA yuppie, vegan, exercise Nazis who was high on stress.

When I pulled up in front of The Chez Dollar Sign I realized the parking valets were nudging one another and laughing at my car. Well I'm not going to give these hyenas the keys to my precious chariot. I did what I usually do. I parked well out of sight and hoofed it. Roughing it up the hill to the restaurant was the most exercise I'd had in years.

Once inside Bob waved me over to his table. The first thing I noticed was Harvey's absence. I sat down and Bob told me, "It's on the studio tab so order whatever you want. I need something to drink. You want any alcohol?"

I was diplomatically humorous. "I try not to drink before dusk Bob."

Bob smiled faintly at my weak joke, and ordered a drink, and he did not stop with one. It suddenly dawned on me why the studio usually sent Harvey with Bob. He was his designated driver. This afternoon it appeared to be my turn. But wait there's more.

Bob's liquid lunch made his tongue wag like a back yard busy body. He began, "Do you know kid I really think you are going to go places with that act of yours? But, never forget how tough this town is. There's a bunch of people in this town who are not exactly who they seem to be."

Bob's speech became even more slurred as he continued. "Take that pretty little red head of yours for instance. I'll bet you're you can't keep your hands off her. But, what do you really know about her? I know something about her you don't. Harvey and I saw her in a strip club in Vegas. She was one of them exotic dancers. Harvey didn't want me to tell you, but I don't want to see you get hurt kid." After noticing my crest fallen expression Bob added, "Look, maybe I shouldn't have said anything."

The following pause was pregnant enough to give birth to quintuplets. I was dumb found. I just couldn't believe it. Once again I had managed to fall in love with yet another woman who could easily rip my heart out and drop kick it through the goal posts of life. If women ever figure out what fragile creatures men really are, divorce court is not the only place we will be sucking the pipe.

At this point besotted even Bob figured out how upset I was. He drunkenly tried to apologize. "Look Jordan everybody has to work at something. Somebody has to strip. Why not a well built little red head named Misty Marlow? Hey it doesn't make her a bad person? In fact she looked pretty damn good to me." Bob finally realized, "I'm not making this any easier for you am I kid?"

Here as a man who could make or break my career. Yet I still had to agree with him. "No Bob you're not, but that's all right. I'm sure I would have found out anyway. Thanks for the lunch, but I think

I'd better drive you back to your office. Come to think of it maybe I should drive you home."

Bob nodded in agreement, because any other body movement might have pitched him to the floor. When we got up, Bob had to throw his arm over my shoulder to steady himself. Then I helped him out to his BMW. While I was driving him home he kept insisting he was all right. I soon realized that my tenuous movie deal hinged on Bob's bad habits. However, on the positive side, I was now dating a sexy Vegas stripper. I immediately drove to Peggy's job at down by the beach, because she was the only one I could talk to at a time like this. Since Peggy hated where she worked and loved to eat it was easy to talk her into a food break, especially with a gossip appetizer. I started right in by unloading the bomb about Erin's being an exotic dancer. Peggy's jaw dropped. She sympathized. "Get out of town! You must be really upset."

"Yeah I guess. It is my belief a woman should only get naked for her husband or anyone willing to pay for a peek."

Peggy mused, "I can't believe you're joking about this Jordan. Are all men's feelings basically a pit stop between sexual fantasies? I would be so furious if this happened to me."

Little did I know across town Erin was discussing this very same topic with her best friend Julie? Erin was wracked with guilt. She confided, "Julie you've known me longer than anybody, but I have never told you or anybody how I was able to finance my law degree. My dad was way too screwed up to even bother with. So I struck out on my own right out of high school. Remember when I moved to Las Vegas and you completely lost track of me? I disappeared on purpose. I set my goals and did what ever it took to make them happen. I changed my name and became an exotic dancer. My Vegas boyfriend Earl even threatened to tell my law firm. Julie I can't bare to let Jordan know, because I'm afraid I might loose him."

Julie interjected, "If you don't tell him you could loose him, especially if he finds out from someone else first. Then he might suspect you are keeping other things from him. You're not are you?"

Back at the beach Peggy was in full lecture mode. I really didn't need her tirade, but nothing could stop her. "Look Jordan what if this is not the only skeleton in this woman's closet. You should talk to her right after work. It's like an open wound. If you let sit it will only fester."

"Hey I'm eating here. I don't need the visual imagery Peggy. Understand I am almost desperate enough to unburden my woes on Travis, but then he would probably just bug me for Erin's phone number. Some guys are like that. There is only one thing left to do."

"I have to call Erin at work and think of some way to ask her if she had been a stripper without offending her." This sounded so stupid I couldn't believe that it had just come out of my own mouth.

After I left Peggy I realized both my personal and professional lives were in some sort of purgatory holding pattern over LAX. Bob is a total drunk.

Erin the ex stripper was all over town with some well-heeled mystery man? At this moment I was headed for a phone booth with my ass in my hands. I dialed Erin's work number. She answered, "Attorney's offices. Erin speaking."

I froze like I had that night on stage except this time there was no magic, no funny jokes, only fear of the unknown. All I could summon up was, "Uh Erin, its Jordan. No I don't need any legal advice yet. I was just with that producer Bob. We were at lunch discussing our film project, but he got so drunk I had to drive him home to sleep it off."

Erin sounded very stressed out. She whispered, "I'm sorry to hear about Bob, but I can't talk right now."

I sensed Erin was not alone in her office. "Your boss is standing right behind you now isn't he?"

Erin responded brusquely, "That's right. I've got to go. Speak with you later."

Why did I have the feeling that T was going to be the one apologizing to her over this? Simply because men are always wrong, just ask any woman.

By the time I got to Erin's that night I realized I had to get her to divulge her past peccadilloes without asking. That was going to involve the skill of a cunning linguist. When Erin opened the door she looked a little anxious. "I thought you were working tonight."

"Tonight at the club maybe I had jokes on my lips, but you were the only thing on my mind Erin."

"Even if you are lying I love hearing it." Erin smiled as she playfully draped her arms around my neck. The instant our lips met I knew any hope of a meaningful dialogue had immediately vanished. My attraction for this woman was so powerful that it frightened me. I couldn't help fantasizing about Erin performing a slow sensual striptease. Is that so wrong? Evidentially not, because that's exactly what she did on our way to her bedroom.

I would have loved asking where she learned to strip like that, but not at the risk of ruining an exquisite night of lovemaking. Not even I'm that stupid. Tonight's intimate tenderness blissfully brought us even closer together. Afterwards we lay there affectionately in one another's arms. Yet Erin still had a concerned look on her face.

My ex-wife taught me to never ask, "Honey what's wrong?" This would invariably get the response; "Oh nothing," or "If you don't know I'm not going to tell you." The final nail in the coffin is, "You really don't want to know," and believe me you don't. Opening that Pandora's box could keep you haggling until dawn without a hint of a solution on the horizon.

Erin began. "There is something I've been meaning to tell you, but I never knew quite where to start. Well you know about my father. He told me my mother died when I was quite young. I would have done anything to get her back, because my dad's abuse was so unrelenting that I took off for Las Vegas after I graduated from high school at sixteen. My dream was always to become a lawyer, but college took a lot more money than I could make as a waitress."

Erin took a deep breath. "I was really taken with the glamour of Las Vegas showgirls, but I wasn't nearly old enough to dance with them. Ever since I was little girl I loved to dance. This club owner saw me boogieing in his club one night and offered me a job. I made more money my first night of exotic dancing than I did in six weeks of waitressing. That's when I met Earl. He was less abusive than my father and sort of took care of me. The longer I went to college the more independent I became. After I was financially able to I moved back to LA. When I graduated from UCLA law school I had hoped to leave the Vegas life and Earl behind me forever. That is when I met you Jordan. Please tell me you're not too upset?"

"No not at all. You did what you had to do." I assured her. Then I held her even closer to show her how little it bothered me.

"I know this was not easy for you Erin, and it does explain Earl. Don't worry sweetheart this isn't even a speed bump in our relationship. I've known ever since our first night together that I was in love with you and your being this honest with me only confirms that emotion."

A tear trickled down Erin's alabaster cheek. "I've always wanted to tell you I loved you too, but I was afraid you'd think I was crazy."

"You must be crazy, because you are in love with a vertically challenged lame joke teller with weird hair. When you could easily be with anybody you wanted to..."

Erin put her finger to my lips and silenced me by saying, "Shush. Don't put yourself down all the time Jordan. From now on that will be my job."

I couldn't believe I had no comeback. I exhaled deeply, because I knew I had finally found a woman who was as intelligent as she was beautiful. I nodded knowingly.

"You are right Erin and I have a feeling you are going to be right a lot from here on out. You know what, I don't think I will mind at all."

Erin smiled as she reached over and kissed me deeply. Then we soared into our sexual stratosphere together. God I loved it when I could fall asleep with her silken body secure in my arms.

The following night at The Comedy Club I walked on stage and embraced the subject of truth in my monologue. After a few opening jokes I launched into this new material. "One of the most elusive qualities in any relationship is the truth. Like when a woman first meets a man she could be thinking, does he own or rent his house and car and will he buy me one too? Sure love is free, but that sex will costs a lot of money. When a man is introduced to a beautiful woman he could be thinking boy she has gorgeous clothes. I wonder if she'll let me wear them later? During lovemaking, when she gets that lustful far away look in her eyes, she could be thinking I wonder what the limit on this moron's gold card is?"

I expounded, "No way you can tell a woman who's obviously lying about her age and weight: oh, you've got to be older and heavier than that. You would find this guy's corpse in an abandoned dumpster in the desert. Sure during sex a man looks like a yak with a groin pull, and his wife has to close her eyes to keep from laughing. Its like not telling your wife the truth when she asks; "Am I the best lover you've ever had?' You can't even pause before you answer that, or you will never have sex with her again. If your wife asks, "Does my butt look too big in this?" You can't say, "Compared to what my pet?" Well you could, but not if she owns a gun. Just like in bed, if you ask her, guess what I've got in my hand for you dear? You don't want to hear, if you can hold it in one hand I ain't interested. See why the real truth is hard to come by? If preachers, politicians, and lawyers always told the truth it would be as stupid as couples being completely honest about their sexual histories. There is some stuff you simply don't need to know especially about the person you share a bed with."

I pointed at a cute girl laughing ringside and said, "She is probably thinking of some freaky-assed sexual escapade she had, and so is her date. Will they share this secret with one another later? Not if either of them ever wants to make love together again."

The young couple laughed and lovingly embraced. I had to admit, "Oh my God they're going to have sex right here and right now. Well there's no way I can follow a live sex act. So thanks for coming folks, and if you didn't come, hey thanks for showing up anyway."

I quickly exited the stage, walked into the crowd, and shook hands with the cute couple. Travis came up and slapped me on the back.

Out of the shadows, Bob's partner Harvey wandered over. Harvey smiled and shook my hand. He enthused, "You were great. Every time I see you perform, you've got a new bit. That's fantastic. I can't wait to tell Bob."

Right now Harvey seemed a little too smarmy even for a Hollywood producer. I couldn't help feeling something was not right so I asked, "Where is Bob?"

Harvey's smile immediately disappeared. He reached out and put his hand on my shoulder and then confided, "Bob had to go back into Betty Ford's for alcohol rehab. He's going to be all right, but the studio really doesn't want to green light this film project without him."

I quickly realized that I was not only loosing my first paying movie deal, but my tenuous cache at the comedy club as well. So I insisted, "There has got to be something we can do. Maybe we could throw him an intervention or something?"

Harvey shook his head and solemnly said, "I know you probably just trying to help. You were being serious weren't you Jordan?"

I grinned sheepishly. "I'm afraid I was. I really want this project to be successful. Travis and I have already written the first draft." This was a ploy to appeal to Harvey's guilt, but hopefully he didn't realize that. Travis knew I was lying. So he shot me a knowing glance. I tried not looking at Travis for fear giving myself away.

Harvey feigned concern then he clapped me on the shoulder. "Don't worry Bob could re-enter the real world tomorrow. Then you can show us what you've written and your hard work won't be for nothing. Well got to go. I'm jetting to the coast in the morning. See you guys." Harvey's exit was so hurried he practically left skid marks on the nightclub floor. Travis and I stood there in a stunned silence, thankful that none of the other comics were within earshot. Travis joked, " On the one hand we're screwed, but on the other, at least we didn't bust our ass writing that damn script."

I was both exasperated and sincere while I proposed, "What have we got to loose by putting this script together ourselves Travis? If Bob does sober up we have something to show him. If he doesn't we can always shop it around. We haven't signed anything yet."

Travis noted, "That'd be great if we ever wrote a script before Jordan, but that just ain't the case. Look man face it, we're right back where we started. Telling jokes to drunks for a living. Why didn't I listen to my pop? He wanted me to go into medicine. Well I kind of did. I sold pot in junior college."

I tried to put a positive spin on things. "Now that is funny Travis. Write it down. By the way, you don't happen to have a joint of that chronic do you? I figured why not get high while witnessing our careers taking a flight to New York? Maybe we could scrounge up a local hell gig and add insult to stonery."

Travis shoved his hand way down in his pocket and fished out a tightly rolled joint. He blew some lint off it and proclaimed, "Damn, it looks like I've got some bud right here dude."

I grabbed a pay phone and after a few calls discovered that a Pacoima club named El Toro Muerto had a couple of fall outs, and could use us. So we took off for the hostility of the inner city.

Travis and I quickly piled into his van outside the club and sped off towards the barrio of East Los Angeles.

I hesitantly took a toke off the joint. "Oh what the hell. Why be depressed? You can't loose a film gig you never really had right?"

Travis toked and joked, "I sure hope we don't get popped. I've got a warrant out on me for going the wrong way in a gay bar."

"And we all know how embarrassing that can be. Give me that damn joint. You are driving."

"We are probably going to be the only gringos at this hell hole? With our luck they'll try to pay us in pesos," joked Travis.

When we pulled up to this seedy Pacoima nightclub we should have know better, because the bouncer was wearing a bulletproof vest. But, were too stoned and depressed to care.

When we entered the club all we saw were bulging muscles, tattoos, and fresh scars; and that was on the women.

It turned out that the most vocal heckler had been recently paroled from prison and she was completely wasted.

The hecklers in this place were so disruptive that the club's MC asked if Travis and me even wanted to go on. Neither of us could figure out which would be more depressing, splitting right now, or trying to get laughs out of this lynch mob?

Travis was pretty baked so he decided to go on next. I warned him, "Travis this heckler is larger, nastier, and more woman than either of one of us. Just like with any wild animal don't show any fear."

My words were to no avail, because the second Travis hit the lip of the stage this huge tattooed broad was on him like roaches on a donut. These were not just insults. They were landing like cruise missiles. How do you respond to taunts like, "You suck! You not funny and you fucking ugly too?"

It was like witnessing a police beating, but Travis bravely pushed on. "All right I suck and I am ugly, but at least I'm not dating you sir."

She furiously screamed, "Fuck you ass face. I'm more woman than you'll ever have, and more man than you will ever be."

When Travis gets nervous his Texas drawl thickens. "Hey you're more man than Janet Reno buddy. Could someone gender test that? God I can't believe I showered for this shit."

This broad was mercilessly. "You showered and you still stink. Get the fuck off stage you chunk of white trash."

Now Travis was really pissed and in a near melt down. "You really shouldn't break those Paxils in half, **sir.** Pound them down with a quart of Jack Daniels if you have to. Slam them damn pills down like they are after-dinner mints. Not a chance in Hell it would make you any fuckin' meaner." Suddenly this mastodon in a dress then drew herself up to her full height, which was about 6'4". After that she started lumbering drunkenly toward the stage.

The vigilant MC alertly leapt on stage to rescue the beleaguered Travis.

He announced, "Let's give it up for Travis Wiley. Come on you know you want to. Our next act can't wait to get up here. Let's hear it for the comedy of Jordan Tyler folks. Don't be shy Jordan. They love you. Come on up."

I guess it was too late to back out now, so I resignedly plodded toward the stage like a dead man walking.

All I could think of was why doesn't a condemned prisoner ask for an automatic weapon and some body armor for a last request? I know I could've used them right now.

I pondered this question while the MC and Travis rudely pushed me on stage. The first words from the mammoth female heckler were, "Look fresh meat! You'd better be funnier than that last asshole boy."

Suddenly I was hit by my own advice. If they smell fear you are road kill. So I knew I had to attack or die. When she yelled, "Look everybody a sawed off little rump ranger." My jokes came out with the precision of automatic gunfire.

I smiled and boldly began. "I can't believe my ex wife followed me to work again tonight. This is why married men would rather hold the remote than their wives. It not only responds when you touch it but, it has a mute button. You can see how tough she is. After sex my ex smoked in bed face down. Tough? She crosses her legs during foreplay. The toughest thing about foreplay with her was haggling over the price. It ain't easy. My wife had spikes on her diaphragm. Do not back up damage will occur. The little woman always wanted to get into an argument and then have sex. How many of you dudes out there have ever been nagged into an erection? I even tried throwing my wife down a wishing well once. Didn't work. She crawled out and beat the shit out of me."

Now even the other women were applauding and laughing. So I pressed on. "I can't believe some people compare marriage to prison. No way. There is sex in jail. Not really good sex, but its there if you want it. Just ask Mike Tyson. But, you know Mike was the husband. Puff Daddy and Robert Downey Jr.

were probably prison bitches. Actually in prison puff daddy is what they do to you. I want a rap name damnit. How about Punk Whitey."

When the crowd started shouting down the big female heckler I interjected, "Great now the crowd is heckling one another, making my job so much easier. Did you know most marriages break up over sex or money? Or in my case paying too much cash for the sex. Hell I've been so lonely lately that I went to a proctologist just for the warmth of his probing rubber glove. How do butt doctors' get in this field, and where was that booth on career day in high school? I'll bet that line was a mighty short. If I wanted to look at assholes the rest of my life I'd become a lawyer or a cop. Why do lawyers' wear their collars up? To hide their foreskins. LA cops are a scary combination too. Minimum wage, high school education, and real bullets. Be glad you live in LA, because in New York the term *police probe' takes on a whole new meaning, and could involve a plunger. It's painful just to say that."

I kept hammering them. "In LA the police cut down on crime the easy way. They eliminated the middleman by sell the drugs themselves. That's why they'll never legalize drugs. Then the LAPD would have to buy their own."

At this point I was slamming. "Cops have no sense of humor. They asked me why I went through a stop sign once? I told them I don't like to read and drive at the same damn time. So they clubbed me, and then they searched my car. I asked him what are you looking for drugs? Oh wow dude you're too late. I like took them all."

Thunderous applause and laughter followed. I couldn't believe that I not only survived, but I had won the crowd over. So I got the hell off stage.

Even the hulking female heckler had been laughing. So figured it was a propitious time for us to grab our cash and bolt for the car.

On our way out, the door was being blocked by a bulky LAPD officer. I remembered that Travis still had that warrant and a half smoked joint on him.

We tried to squeeze by the cop, but couldn't. He loomed ominously over us and had to notice how uncomfortable we were. Policemen must love this power. Why else put up with all that grief from the dregs of society like us? Travis and I froze for a second. Then the officer broke into a smile. He extended a hand and said, "Nice show. Loved the cop stuff." We thanked him and then slowly backed out of the club, just as the hulking female heckler was drunkenly lurching towards me for a big make up hug.

As we fled to Travis's van we got congratulatory shout outs in both Spanish and English. We responded with thanks yous and mochas gracious.

Once securely inside Travis's van we sped to the freeway and headed home. I couldn't help but notice Travis's sullen mood. I thought I knew why, but I was afraid of further upsetting him. So we sat in a stony silence except for the gasps and sputters of his air-cooled engine. Finally Travis sarcastically pointed out, "That went real good didn't it?"

At first I didn't know how to respond, but it didn't stop me from asking, "Are you kidding me? We were lucky to escape that toilet without any serious flesh wounds."

Travis exploded. "You did great. They fucking hated me."

I tried being sympathetic. "Hate is such a strong word. They just misunderstood you Travis. It happens to every comic."

Travis was wallowing in the depths of own despair. "If you hadn't jumped on stage and laid waste Bigfoot in a bra, her tire tracks would be across my ass right now. I didn't even get a shot at being average. I blew major chunks up there, and you had to save my ass yet again. I should be obliged, but I fucking hated it. I'm tired of **you** always bailing **me** out just to make **us** look good."

I knew I had to alleviate his pain without causing any further psychic damage. "It could have just as easily happen to me Travis."

"But it didn't, **God damnit!** It happened to **me,"** he burst out.

"And it also happened to every comic who went on before you tonight. They even hated the MC and he spoke Spanish. Nobody's a hit every damn night. God even bombs now and again or Arkansas, Alabama, and Louisiana would be mostly unpopulated."

"Good point buddy." Thank God Travis finally chuckled.

I was so relieved. "And I am your buddy. In fact if you guys hadn't pushed me on stage tonight my own insecurities would have opened up a complete can of whoop-ass on me. Let's never do another bathroom like that one, no matter how desperate, depressed, or stoned we are. What we need now is a road trip."

Travis smiled. "Thanks for the remind. Looks like we got more herb right here." He then reached into his pocket and lit the half smoked joint.

I confessed, "The way our fate has been lately don't you think we should wait until we get home before you fire that up?"

Just then from right behind us a cop siren wailed out. Red and blue cop lights had us lit up like a Christmas tree, and Travis was freaking out.

He quickly shoved the large roach back in his pocket. "Oh God please let me skate on this and I'll do anything you want! Oh shit! What am I gonna do if he checks me for warrants man?"

I joked, "What if he frisks me Travis and I like it? He could make me submit to a cavity search. You know I'm a sucker for a man in uniform."

When the patrol car pulled up next to our van Travis was sweating like a fat boy at a buffet table. Now both were loosing it. Then the cop car pulled out and around, and promptly busted the car right in front of ours.

Normally you'd feel sympathy for a person who is less fortunate than you, but not when it's your own bacon being saved. I was really relieved just to see a smile on Travis's face. So we immediately burst out laughing. Then we both high fived, and missed.

"See Travis out luck is changing already. Maybe we should go home and start on that script, just in case Harvey comes back from New York and wants to see it. Maybe Bob will even get out of re-hab."

Travis pined, "What can I write about. I never wrote nothing in my life. I don't even get off a Christmas cards on time."

"How hard can it be? It's television. We can write about tonight's gig. We can write about all the hot looking women in LA who can't wait to date two broke-ass unemployed comics."

Travis stopped me cold. "Hey you got a babe. Only upside to my sex life is you can't get your hand knocked up. But, you got a hot looking red head. How'd you pull that off anyway Jordan?"

"I believe pulling it off is her job, but thanks for asking."

"You ain't going to wise-ass your way out of this one Jordan. I want some particulars about you and big red and I want 'em now," Travis insisted.

"Sorry. I don't kiss and tell."

Travis insisted, "Look Jordan. Tonight I just got stomped by a crowd so dumb they'd go to pornos for the plot. I'm flat broke, and I couldn't get laid in a woman's prison with a fist full of smokes. So you'd better kiss and tell right now buddy, or I'll drop your ass off here in the middle of Compton."

Even thought Travis was probably kidding, I knew I'd better pacify him with some ripe relationship tidbits, because we had just passed a Compton off ramp. I began by telling him about my encounter with Earl, when he smashed Erin's cell phone. Travis was amazed. "I didn't know you had the balls to back down a whack job like that. Then you jammed your hand in your pocket like you had a gun. That was pure genius. I guess red must be worth dying for."

I exclaimed, "Oh my God! That's why Earl split in such a hurry? Now that big son of a bitch thinks I'm armed. Is that a good thing?"

Travis admitted, "It's better than him thinking you're a pussy. Speaking of pussy."

I was indignant. "You are probably not going to be satisfied unless I break out a video of Erin and me getting it on are you?"

Travis smiled lecherously, "You mean you got it on tape?"

(Erin's dream.) Erin envisions my bedroom and me making passionate love to a woman whose face is obscured by the shadows of the room. Suddenly my bedroom door burst open and in walked Erin. I sat bolt upright in bed. Neither Erin nor I could hide the shock of our embarrassment. Erin fled out of the room in tears, and I sat there too stunned to move.

In her own bed at home Erin shot bolt upright. Hot tears streamed down her face as she reluctantly reached for the phone and punched in a number.

It was almost 2AM when Erin woke Peggy up. Her grogginess was apparent. "I'm sorry Peggy. I was worried about Jordan. Did I wake you up?"

Peggy mumbled, "Don't worry. I had to get up to answer the phone anyway. Who is this? Oh Erin. I think Jordan is out playing some club with Travis. I didn't hear him come in yet, but I am pretty out of it right now."

Erin began reluctantly, " I had this very disturbing dream about Jordan." It's not just an irrational fear of mine. I have lost people who were very close to me. Now I am falling for Jordan and that old fear is rearing its ugly head again."

"That's interesting," yawned Peggy. "What was the dream about?"

Erin was silent for a moment then answered. "There is no other way to put this. I caught Jordan in bed with another woman. Then I ran out of the bedroom and he didn't even try to stop me. Jordan just sat there in bed with that other woman."

Peggy could barely keep her eyes open. "I don't know what to say Erin. Are you really afraid Jordan is going to cheat on you?"

"I don't know. I hope not."

"Believe me Erin the way Jordan feels about you I am sure it will never happen."

Erin seemed relieved. "Thanks Peggy. I really needed to hear that. I'm sorry I disturbed you with my paranoia. I'm sure you have a lot better things to do right now. Don't tell Jordan I called. OK? OK Peggy? Peggy are you still there?"

The next thing Erin heard was the loud rumble of Peggy's snoring into the phone. She chuckled and gently hung up the receiver.

That following night when I met Erin at her house she seemed stressed out for no apparent reason. All I told her was, "I don't like this any more than you do honey, but Travis and I have to go on the road right now to make any real money."

"Why can't you play local clubs like the one last night?"

I tried not to roll my eyes in disbelief when I explained, "You don't make squat playing those in town clubs. To make a decent living in LA you either have to be working in a movie or in a TV series. As a comic they only pay you well when you leave town. It sucks, but I didn't make up the rules."

Erin's sarcastic response was, "I can only imagine how much you hate being on the road. You come off stage in little nowhere town and some strange drunken bar babes struts over to you. Then she starts shoving her phone number and God knows what else in your face. It must be awful."

My first mistake was trying to counter with logic. "Erin it's not like I'm a rock star or something. Women don't exactly throw themselves at short, goofy looking 37-year-old comic."

Erin looked directly into my eyes. "Why not? I did."

I hoped exactly the right words would come out of my mouth next, to make her feel better about me taking off on the road. "I know you did and that's why I love you sweetheart. Believe me I would never do anything to jeopardize what we have Erin."

When she looked disconsolate for a second I was concerned. Then she snuggled close to me for a long warm embrace.

I couldn't believe I might have actually said the right thing for a change. I guess men can learn from their mistakes after all.

That night our lovemaking reached make-up sex magnitude, but I couldn't shut my brain off. Was our relationship headed to the next level? Were we going from love to trust? Would I be able to handle the next level of intimacy? Then it hit me that I was questioning my own pleasure. Perhaps I was experiencing doubt, because I felt this love was just too good to last. I have to learn how to accept pure love and incredible sex the moment it is presented. I could easily blame religion for this.

Not just one religion is responsible for sexual guilt, all of them are. I really have to learn to relax when I'm in bed with Erin.

Just as we drifted off to sleep in each other's arms Erin's phone rang. She answered it in a stilted cryptic manner, and then didn't tell me who it was.

When I finally slipped off to sleep, I hoped the next level in our relationship would be mutual trust.

I arrived at Peggy's place the next morning with love in my loins, but uncertainty in my heart. I could hardly believe it when Travis was waiting there for me. I had to ask, "What are you doing vertical before noon?"

His answer was even more surprising. "I was up all night working on our script buddy. What you been doing Jordan? Or should I say who?"

I was so worried about Erin's late night call I could barely muster a grin through my sarcasm. "I suppose that is your idea of humor? I only hope what you've written is equally as clever Travis."

Travis's reaction was predictable. "Ouch! Has the sidewinder of sarcasm has had a lover's squabble already?"

I warned him, "Look Travis we both had a long night. Lighten up. Oh what the heck come on inside and show me what you've written."

I had never seen Travis this excited about anything that wasn't wearing a skirt. So once inside I poured over his barely legible notes.

"This is all about me. I guess I should be thankful you didn't fabricate any of the intimate parts of my sex life."

Travis's grin broadened. "Oh I did. You wouldn't give me the skinny on you and Erin. So I just made shit up. If you want to lay the real deal on me now is the time."

"Look Travis just because you wouldn't have a sex life without X-rated videos is no reason to rely on me as your local porn merchant."

"I'm sorry man, but you know sex sells. I could have lied about some hot dream babe drooling over me."

"You're right. I suppose a chapter on the joy of masturbation would not exactly be a sales point. At best it is beating around the bush. The best thing about your auto erotic sex life is that it is quick, cheap, and easy."

"Kind of like you Jordan."

"And, you always know who's going to finish first Travis. You." I added this swiftly to avoid any further discussion about Erin or me.

There was no way I could tell him about all of my insecurities regarding Erin. So I circumvented the topic. "We are going to have to manufacture something about my love life. Erin and I are getting along fine. Maybe it's time to find you a woman Travis. How about my roommate Peggy?"

Travis knew she and I were best of friends, but that didn't prevent him from teasing. "You got to be kidding. She's big enough to bench press my skinny butt. Of course you would have to spot me Jordan."

Despite myself I went along with his mockery. "Come on Travis don't sell big women short. If you fall out of bed they can drag you right back in. If the car breaks down screw it. Let them push if they want equality."

Travis wouldn't stop. "If we ever did the nasty, she would have to get on top? I got a real bad back."

We were on roll until Peggy walked in. "What's so funny," she demanded?

Travis and I stopped laughing long enough to lie in unison. "Oh nothing."

"You were talking about me weren't you?"

He and I were so guilty about the laughing, we had to leave the room. I guaranteed her, "It was not about you Peg. It's this script we are working on."

Peggy's prickly response was, "Since when did you two learn how to write?"

"Wait a darned minute Peggy. Travis here can write real good."

"Yeah right. Look I am tired and hungry. Jordan what do we have in the fridge that you two haven't picked over yet?"

"There is some unopened airline food from my last road gig. Knock yourself out Peggy."

"I can't believe I'm asking this, but how long has it been in the fridge?"

I yelled from the other room. "Airline food has about the same shelf life as brake fluid. Bon appetite." Then I addressed myself to Travis's notes. I insisted, "Travis you really have to put more of yourself in this story."

"Yours is a lot better. My life ain't worth spit. I figured if people wanted to learn more about the wide wonderful world of white trash they'd watch "Cops" or "Jerry Springer." Travis modestly admitted.

I was both moved and flattered. "Travis you're my friend. You have to be in this script. What would Groucho be without Harpo, Abbot without Costello, Laurel without Hardy, Firestone tires without Ford?"

When Travis said, "Archie Bunker without the Meathead;" we both smiled and then we went back to work on the script. We didn't even take notice that it had gotten dark outside until Travis asked, "You think Peggy left any of that airline food or is that a dumb question?" Without hesitation he reached for the phone and dialed a number. He spoke into the receiver, "Is this Domino's pizza?"

With a half finished script in our hands, as well as no money in our pockets Travis and I ventured out of town on the comedy circuit. I couldn't forget how I had lost Noella after my last big road trip. So it was not without trepidation that I departed from my new found love Erin.

It seems that life is a series of tests, and this was like an unscheduled pop quiz on the meaning of trust. When I first called Erin from the road both of us discovered how much we missed one another. We figured it was either love, extreme loneliness, or both.

One of our stops was Travis's home state of Texas. The women there loved him and he loved them right back. Sure a few local girls approached me. They inquired, "You all ain't from around her are ya?" My answer was always, "No, but have you met my friend Travis? He's from Lubbock." Oddly enough this kept us both out of trouble. There were times I called when Erin wasn't there and I'd start to freak out, but Travis was always able to pacify me with a tranquilizer dart of his homespun humor.

At one Dallas gig this cute cowgirl heckled Travis mercilessly. After the show she bought him a drink, and then took him home with her.

Soon Travis realized what a vapid empty experience sex on the road really was. On the bright side, it did seem to conquer his fear of hecklers.

One night we ate out with the same cowgirl who had taken Travis home. I couldn't believe how much food she could shove in her mouth at one time. Which only prompted Travis to tell me what else she could cram. This only caused him to lament, "Why can I find honeys like this back in Los Angeles?"

After two months of grueling road gigs we wearily dragged ourselves back to LA. Sure we made money, and Travis did finally understand the healing powers of humping a heckler. We had also compiled a complete script about the humorous vicissitudes of life on the road of comedy.

When we got to Peggy's place I teased him about all the motel towels and shampoos he had stolen. Travis insisted, "Everybody takes them. Now you rip off a Bible or a TV, then you're pond scum."

While we had been gone Erin helped Peggy drop some thirty-five pounds. She looked like a whole new woman. Peggy now swore by her revolutionary weight loss program. All she did was stop slamming down junk food, and started exercising. I asked Peggy, "All you had to do was eat a carrot and do some sit ups? Why couldn't I have thought of that?" Realizing my sarcasm, she cursed and hurled a can of Slim Fast at me. It was clear that weight loss and her temper were two separate issues. I rushed up for a congratulatory hug before she could throw anything else at me.

When Peggy hugged me back it almost snapped three of my ribs.

The most amazed person in the room was good old Travis. He was smiling from ear to ear and Peggy smiled right back at him. I remembered the same look in Travis's eyes whenever he met a woman he really liked. My mind raced into the future. Could I handle the thought of my two best friends doing the horizontal tango, or was it just too creepy? Sure I want them both to be happy, but the thought of them having sex was almost as disgusting as catching your parents touching one another.

What if I walked in on them doing it on top the kitchen table? I swear I'd have to hose them both down, and I could never eat off that kitchen table again.

Travis and I took off for The Comedy Club that same night. On the way Travis couldn't wait to discuss Peggy's transformation. "Can you believe how awesome Peggy looked? She was lookin' at me pretty good too. Peggy's got to be the only babe in LA to gawk at my butt without checking for that lump of cash in my rear pocket first."

I laughed and was creeped out the same time.

"That is just the type of stuff you should put in your act. Travis. But, please try to remember Peggy is my best friend."

"Why can't I be hot for Peggy? Shouldn't we get the same shot at scorchin' the sheets as you do?"

I guess he was right, but it still bothered me.

I conceded, "Go ahead and tell Peggy how you feel, as long as you think you can handle her. Remember if it doesn't work out don't come to me for advice."

"Oh that's what you're worried about? I figured you were thinking I'm not good enough for her."

"My folks didn't think I was good enough for anybody, but it never stopped me from dating my sister," Travis joked.

"You are one bad mother fu," I began.

"Shut your mouth," added Travis.

"I'm just talking about Travis." We both laughed at our "Shaft" homage. Internally I continued to wrestle with the thought of Travis lunging after Peggy, and if I were about to become the Dear Abby in little this tryst?

I snapped out of my thoughts in time to shout, "Don't pass The Comedy Club Travis. Why not do up both a favor and park your vintage van around back. At least that way we can pretend to be successful comics. You didn't happen to bring a copy of our script did you?"

"Sure, but we still don't know if Bob sobered up yet. Harvey ain't called has he," Travis queried?

As we walked towards the comedy club I admitted. "I tried to contact Harvey when we were on the road. He has a service, a pager, call forwarding, and voice messaging into the after life; but mysteriously enough no one in LA ever returns a damn phone call."

When we strolled passed a bank on Sunset Blvd. Travis observed, "Look Jordan there are a couple of hookers standing next to one of them ATM machines. Great! Now I got to wait in two lines to get screwed."

I laughed. "You must have gotten a comedy injection on our last road trip Travis." When we walked into The Comedy Club it was as if time had stood still.

The same comics were sucking up to the management. Similar acts were either killing or bombing, and we had to wade through all of them to get stage time. Fortunately both of us, were in too good a mood to care.

Now I had to figure what was ticking me off enough to do new jokes about, because there didn't seem to be anybody here tonight who wanted to hire a middle aged out of work comic.

Our good mood soon deteriorated. Barry, the club's owner, wouldn't let us go on until it was so late the crowd was completely smashed. The wasted hecklers were actually encouraging one another. Since he was going on next, Travis was having a paranoid Pacoima flashback. He was even bumming me out.

I tried giving him some confidence. "Travis there are no industry people here, so no pressure. Don't let them know you care and you'll be fine."

The minute Travis stepped on stage he spotted Bob and Harvey walking in, and they sat right down in front. Travis's eyes widened visibly. He stood stock still for what seemed like an eternity. Then the first heckler blind-sided him. "Say something funny or let the next asshole on stage?"

Travis began gamely. "Please sir not now. I'm really depressed tonight. My Doberman was just killed by a Chihuahua. Yeah it got stuck in his throat." He got his first laugh so he kept on moving.

"I hate Chihuahua's. They ain't dogs they're rats that bark. "Yip-yip-yip. Just drop kick them little suckers through the goal posts. Boom! Three points. Put them in a microwave and give them to a Korean family down the block for a snack. Puncture them first so you don't screw up a perfectly good microwave."

Travis smiled. "Yeah that's sick. Not as sick as my girlfriend wanting me to walk her Pekinese. She told me to be careful, because it was a rare Chinese dog. I told her that any dog that made it out of China was pretty damn rare, or medium rare." Travis was on such a roll that even the drunks loved him. He pointed at the drunkest heckler. "You are sick sir. You're the type of dude who would park in a handicap zone with a bike rack on your car. Admit it. You would take Stevie Wonder to a sunset. You're sick. You'd give a jet ski to a. one armed guy just to see him run around in circles like this." Travis mimed a one-armed guy jet skiing in circles around the mike stand.

Travis then went in for the kill. "No matter how sick you all are, do not let your pets in the room when you are having sex. What do dogs like to do? Watch. Like they are taking doggie notes, to use out on the front lawn with their bitches? Roof-roof! Roll over and let's do it people style. Try it you'll like it sir."

Travis enthused, "Cats are different. They have to get **involved.** They will crawl right up between you and your woman lick your face. Either that or they will aim claws down for your naked ass just as you are about to climax. MEOWWW! Kick little fluffy against the curtains, because a good orgasm is hard to come by, but a friggin' cat is real easy to find." This routine brought the audience to whole other level of laughter and thunderous applause. Travis innately understood that this was his cue to exit triumphantly. So he bowed deeply and split. Backstage Travis admitted to me that he had just gotten one of his most valuable lessons in nightclub comedy. He discovered that hecklers were just drive by assholes without a stage or a microphone. They were only after the same attention we are.

I pointed out, "Like that cowgirl heckler in Dallas? If I remember correctly she gave you some real hands-on attention."

"Well it did stop her from heckling me again didn't it?" Travis reminded me.

"Of course it did. It's not polite to talk with your mouth full."

As we both laughed at my stupid joke, Barry the owner followed us backstage. "You think that shit you did with the heckler was pretty fucking funny huh Travis?" Barry admonished.

"It got laughs Barry." Travis responded defensively.

"Yeah and it got complaints too. That heckler happened to be blind, and if it ends up costing me business you're history Travis. By the way Jordan, you got bumped tonight. My kid Matt needs some stage time." Barry's words were as fetid as the cigar smoke encircling him. He scowled one last time at us, and then slithered out of the backstage area.

I noticed that Travis's mood had plummeted from elation to despair. So I joked, "Barry has got to be the only guy I know who could bum out the sun. Don't worry Travis, it's only the boss man trying to keep us hired hands down."

Both our faces brightened when Harvey walked backstage accompanied by Bob. Bob said, "Surprise boys I escaped from Betty Ford. Which is more than you can say for her husband Gerald. Harvey mentioned that you guys have a script for me." Travis produced a copy of our rough draft and handed it to him. Bob continued, "This is only a rough draft are you sure it is all right if I take this copy?"

Travis nodded yes. "Sure Bob. Good to see you back."

Harvey added, "When I left for New York I thought this whole project was dead on arrival. Then Bob returned, and the studio told us we were back in business." They both smiled and shook our hands.

Bob assured us by saying; "If these pages are half as funny as Travis was tonight we will be talking some big money real soon. Sorry we can't stay, but Harvey and I got an early call tomorrow morning."

When Travis and I left The Comedy Club, Harvey and Bob were busy talking to Barry and his son Matt. Because of the way Barry had chastised Travis, this didn't set too well with him. "I don't trust that little weasel," muttered Travis.

"Which one Barry or his son? Not to worry Travis you are funny, where as his kid Matt will always be comedy challenged."

"When did no talent ever stop Barry from putting his kid on stage?" Scoffed Travis.

"In fact when did having no aptitude ever prevent nepotism? How else could you possibly explain the presidency of George W. Bush? Proof that there is no accounting for tastes in America. Favoritism is as old as the sands of time. Young comics always ask me what it takes to become a star. I tell them family in the business. If your dad the head of a studio, a network, or named Spelling, you probably have a shot. It must be nice to make money the old fashioned way by inheriting it, huh Travis? Why didn't we put that in our script too?"

"Because, we want to work in this town again? Screw this negative crap. You've got a good-looking red head waiting for you, and a we just wrote a damn funny script."

"Wait a minute did you forget that you've got Peggy, Travis?"

"Jordan I got nothing. Peggy doesn't know I'm hot for her, and I don't know how to tell her. She's your friend Jordan you tell her," Travis insisted.

I shook my head no and told him, "I'm not going to be your Cyrano Travis. You have to talk to her yourself. I will invent a reason to not be home at he time. That way you two can be alone with your salacious little desires."

"I don't know what that means, but sounded real dirty. I like that. Look at it this way Jordan. Peggy will either let me do things to her that I have not even tried on myself, or she'll smack the crap out of me."

"So either way you'll be turned on right Travis? Sounds like a win-win to me."

On our way home I came to this realization. Love can either lull you into a blissful sense of security; or it can shut off other important parts of your brain like common sense. Then you let your guard down. It can be a good thing when you fall into the comfortable lap of unconditional love. Hopefully this was where Erin and I were headed.

However, when it came to Peggy, Travis didn't have a clue where he was going, but I'll bet she will let him know in a heartbeat.

The next day Travis came over to Peggy's place. He had finally summoned the courage to ask her out. "Peggy would go out with me? I know I ain't much to look at, but I do put out."

"So you think you are a good lover? Is that it Travis?"

Travis joked, "I should be. I get a lot of practice at home alone."

Peggy ultimately went out with Travis, because of his sense of humor. Her conditions were that she could pick out the restaurant and Travis's wardrobe. She asked him, "How do you figure out what to wear before you leave the house Travis?"

"The way most guys do. I give my clothes a quick sniff and if they don't stink too bad, I just throw them on," admitted Travis.

"So the hamper is basically a recycle bin to you, right Travis?"

"What's in tarnation is a hamper?"

"Never mind. Let's get you into something decent looking so we can go out to dinner."

Travis was actually relieved, because the only major embarrassment left would be if she wanted to go dancing. He figured that dancing was a vertical expression of a horizontal desire for women, but not for men from Texas. Travis knew there was no sexual expression in square or line dancing. There couldn't be, or they wouldn't be yelling out the steps to you while you're trying to square dance. However, he did tell Peggy he got orders like that once during sex. The first thing Peggy asked Travis was, "After dinner can we go dancing? I love a man who can move well on the floor."

Travis tried to worm out of it by explaining, "I hate to tell you this, but most guys who I've seen dance real good are usually dancing with other men."

This did not stop Peggy from wanting to test his theory, or the possibility of opposites attracting.

What could possibly be more opposite than men and women to begin with? Well Travis and Peggy of course. She was a big, bossy, Baltimore native. Travis was a California cowboy by way of Texas. Erin and I agreed that this was truly a match made anywhere but in Heaven. On the up side we noticed when they left the house together, that Travis and Peggy were about the same height.

Evidentially their dinner and dancing date went better than expected. Neither Erin nor I heard from them for three days. When I tried to reach Peggy I discovered she had called in sick for work. In fact I was about to contact the police, until I spotted a TV news report about a casino heist in Las Vegas. Right there on the surveillance video of the robbery was Peggy and Travis having a drink in the casino. I was still in shock when the phone rang. "Hello Travis? We've been worried sick about you. Yeah I know where you are. You and Peggy just made the channel 4 evening news. You were celebrating what? No I'm already sitting down. You and Peggy got married? Sure I'm OK with it if that is what you both want. Sure it is kind of sudden. Why do you have to be questioned by the Vegas police before you can leave? You didn't rob the place. Did they get your money too? Peggy wouldn't give them her purse. That's my girl. All right she is your girl now. Yeah I heard the other line beeping too. Just get home safely. Bye."

I punched the call-waiting button. "Hello Erin? You're not going to believe this, but Peggy and Travis are in Las Vegas. You saw them on the news too? Get this. They got married by a Wayne Newton impersonator. I guess the best man was Sigfried, and Roy gave the bride away. Come on how can I not joke? My two best friends just got married in Vegas on their first date. You know my motto is I mock therefore I am."

"You want me to come over right now?" All right. See you in a few honey."

As I left for Erin's something didn't feel right. While pulling out of my driveway two guys riding a garbage truck sniggered at my car. Then a nun cut me off on the freeway and gave me the finger. Was this some sort of a sign or what?

When I arrived Erin opened the door and appeared as enchanting as ever. "Do you want something to drink," she purred? Erin handed me a glass of wine. Then she held me closely and gazed directly into my eyes. Erin's intoxicating effect on me was down right addictive. At this point she could have asked for the world. My only question would have been how do you want it wrapped sweetheart? My big problem was that my attraction to Erin was so intense that it often left me tongue-tied. How could I put my feelings for her in just the right words?

"Sweet Erin. Shall I compare thee to a summer's day? Thou art hot, sweet, and sticky." Was not exactly what I had in mind.

Erin giggled at my lame attempt at mixed metaphors. Then she admitted, "Jordan you are the only person I know who would try to combine a Shakespeare sonnet with a rock and roll lyric."

"Sorry Erin. I am a comic. Even my purloined poetry has punch lines."

Erin wisely put an hors d'oeuvres in my mouth, before I could say anything else that would completely destroy the magic of the moment. She always knew how to do exactly the right thing to heighten our passion for one another. Most women will let you know what they want, but men have difficulty turning off their testosterone long enough to hear them.

As soon as we were soaring to yet undiscovered heights of sexual bliss I couldn't help thinking why women put up with men in the first place.

I was convinced that if anyone ever invented a vibrator that would cuddle after sex, calls the next day, and pays the rent; men would become obsolete. Then I thought maybe I should write that down; but that would've been rude, especially during foreplay. Besides, her dog Eli was watching us from the end of the bed. Then I remembered Travis's bit about dogs watching humans having sex. I barely kept myself from cracking up.

Afterwards we lay there bathed in the warmth of post coital pleasure. Then Erin said the one thing that is even more chilling to men than an IRS audit. "Jordan we have to talk." Women invariable take advantage of that languid moment right after sex to ask us vital information. They know full well that the blood is nowhere near our brain at that time. There isn't enough blood in the body for both organs.

H3

I should've started snoring, but I was too late. Instead my foolish response was, "Couldn't we please talk about this in the morning or perhaps the early afternoon?"

I felt Erin's body tense up. I was immediately aware that this was not what she wanted to hear.

When she turned her back on me I knew I was in serious trouble. I had to ask, "Sweet heart is something wrong?" Both of us lay there anxiously waiting for the second cliché to drop

I couldn't believe I was only two body jerks away from a deep sleep when Erin shook me and demanded, "Don't fall asleep on me now Jordan. I need to know where you think our relationship is headed?"

Boy was I awake now. This must have been how Doc Holiday felt when he was ambushed at the O.K. Corral. The big difference being that I was completely unarmed and sober.

I answered anyway. "Right now I feel like I'm in love with the most incredible woman I have ever been with."

She held me at arms length and firmly stated, "Saying you love me is one thing Jordan. Showing me is what really counts right now."

I insisted, "I have shown you haven't I? Remember who protected you from that thug ex-boyfriend who crushed your cell phone. Earl wanted to make both of us kiss the concrete?"

"I appreciated that Jordan, but I can't shake the feeling you are not always going to be there for me. Your suitcase is like you are. It is always packed and ready to leave town at a moments notice. I need more then that. I'm not just some ex-stripper you picked up in a nightclub. I have to know that I am not simply a convenience that is here just you when you feel like sleeping with someone."

Erin was adamant as she spoke. Now both of us were disappointed, but for an entirely different reasons.

Erin finally let me hold her and I never wanted to let go. However, I understood that would only happen at the cost of my precious freedom. So I knew my next words would be crucial. This did not stop me from blurting out, "We could move in together, and I'll try to keep the road trips to a minimum."

Erin quickly added, "Then we could shop for an engagement ring together?"

I couldn't help thinking maybe it was time to settle down, live responsibly, and be unhappy for a while. Like I'd be any more miserable than I was before I met Erin. Women had been turning me down all day every day. Yet I still hoped to stave off the inevitable by asking her, "Why is this so important all of the sudden sweetheart?"

"Because, now I know that you are the man I want to spend the rest of my life with," she answered resolutely.

Now I wondered how it was possible to be so completely in love with this woman and still be reluctant to be with her until death do us part? Death? Couldn't we settle for a permanent crippling injury? Death is so darn final. I chuckled at this joke I had written directly after my bitter divorce.

Erin snapped me out of my thoughts by asking, "Jordan what are you thinking right now? Does that chuckling mean you agree with me?"

How can the idea of marrying the woman of your dreams resemble a cell door clanging shut? And, was it possible to tell Erin how I felt without revealing how marriage phobic I was?

Instead I naively asked, "Honey shouldn't we give ourselves a little more time to think about this?"

Erin frowned. "You are joking right?"

"You know me. Always trying to make the world safe for humor." I immediately realized that any hope of a continued relationship Erin would now involve some unbelievably fancy footwork, or a ring. I should have said let's go to a jewelry store right now sweetheart. But what actually came out was, "Sure we can move in together whenever you want."

It must have been the right thing to say, because Erin bent over and kissed her dog flush on the lips. Then without wiping it off she leaned in and kissed me. This is great. I'm moving in and the dog is the first one to get kissed on the lips. I felt married already and it was scaring the hell out of me.

On the other hand Erin was ecstatic. "I can't wait to tell my friends Jordan. Let's get an antique engagement ring tomorrow. If it was good luck for somebody else it will be for us too."

I tried to lamely explain, "Erin honey I meant we should live together first to see if it works out."

Erin exploded, "You **what!** You expect to just move in here, eat my food, have sex, and come and go as you damn well please? I'll tell you what, hold on to that little fantasy while you're putting your clothes on and getting the HELL out of my house."

Then she shoved me off her bed onto the floor. I almost landed on her dog Eli, who was as surprised as I was. I hadn't seen a mood swing like this since Linda Blair in "The Exorcist". She continued to scream, "Get out and leave me alone! I thought this was going to be the most special night of my life. Instead you ruined it." I reached for her and she yelled, "DON'T TOUCH ME!"

Erin threw my clothes at me as I retreated into the living room. I tried to explain myself.

"Erin please try to understand that I haven't even been divorced for a year. It only makes sense to be sure it will work out first? You've got to know how much I really care for you?"

Erin's rage was so intense she didn't seem to hear me at all. When she shoved me out of the front door in to the street I was a disheveled mess, and only half dressed. She shouted after me, "Don't ever come back here again!" As the slammed door echoed in my ears, I had never felt so alone in all my life.

I shuffled to my poor little car and crawled in. Then without warning hot tears welled up in my eyes and streamed down my face.

It suddenly hit me that my stupid fear of marriage was costing me the most incredible woman I'd ever been with. A ring and a lousy piece of paper is what stood between Erin's and my happiness. I felt like a complete idiot.

When I got back to Peggy's she agreed that yes I was indeed a complete idiot. She was amazed. "How could you let a woman like Erin get away? She is everything you have been looking for. Sometimes I don't understand you at all Jordan. I know you were badly burned by your ex wife, but Erin is not her. I know this woman really loves you. She told me so."

Peggy noticed my crestfallen appearance. So she assured me, "Don't worry I'll call her in the morning. We will have lunch and talk. I only want to see you both as happy as Travis and me. Right now I've got to get some sleep. Some of us have to work in the morning." Then she shuffled back into her bedroom and closed the door.

I figured as long I was too depressed to sleep, I may as well put my life in danger by walking the mean streets of Los Angeles. When I left our place the first person I came across was a homeless man pushing his cart. I couldn't help thinking; well at least I'm not that poor guy. Then I saw a young woman retreating and yelling at her boyfriend. He was imploring her to come back. Immediately I realized I could easily be that guy. I looked skyward as if for Devine intervention. That didn't happen so I kept on walking west towards the ocean.

My journey eventually brought me down to my favorite beach near the pier in Santa Monica.

The brilliant red sun peeking over LA's morning haze only served to remind me of that bright red Irish light now missing in my own life. Erin was the symphony of my soul and yet I could not express the right words to convince her of that. Not without a ring and a wedding.

How ironic. I could mesmerize an entire room full of strangers from a hostile comedy stage, and even get them to like me; but could not perform similar magic on the woman I loved. What in God's name was wrong with me?

I would love to tell Erin that I wanted our relationship to heal the cracks in our hearts and love all the hurt away, even if it is a stolen lyric from an 80's love song. What genius bon mot did I come up with? I muttered, "Sweet Erin shall I compare thee to a summer's day, thou art hot sweet and sticky. Damn, when I need the poetry of words the most, they completely elude me."

As I rambled on to myself, I passed a frail bearded Asian man doing his Tai Chi at the beach. He grinned at me and then uttered, "You just combined a Shakespeare and Sammy Hagar quote didn't you?"

"Sorry, I didn't realize I was mumbling out loud. Hope I didn't disturb you sir."

"A well timed remark, especially when it's funny, is never a disturbance," he replied. "You look troubled my son. Is it a woman, money, or both?" The old man rhythmically continued performing his Tai Chi.

I looked around for any hidden cameras, because this was LA. "Are you a psychic or something? And, yes it does happen to be a woman, but I don't have the enough money to buy her a decent ring anyway."

His penetrating gaze seemed to pierce my very soul. Then he replied, "If she truly loves you she would accept a ring out of a Cracker Jack box."

"It's not the money that counts. It is your reluctance to commit to her that has cause you both despair." His fluid movements were as poetic as his prophecy.

"Man you are good. How did you know that?" I was stunned.

He studied me for a minute then replied, "Your face is not reflecting anger. So it's not something she did to you. Instead you appear remorseful. That means it's undoubtedly something you did or failed to do."

"You are incredible. Have you ever thought of going on TV and making money doing this?"

The old man shook his head in disbelief. "You're not listening to your heart. Life is not just about money. Neither is your problem. It's about knowing what's inside your heart, and trusting yourself enough to share it with others. A good example is that man in the business suit walking down there by the ocean. He is a big Hollywood studio lawyer who was just fired by his brother in law. Then he lost all faith in himself, and his wife left him. He thought it was all about the money too."

"How do you know all that? Just by looking at this guy's body posture. Did you feel his vibes, read his aura, or what?

The old man mused. "It is not difficult to access the messages of the soul if you embrace the silence of the moment."

"That is it? All you had to do was be silent and you were privy to all that poor guy's problems?"

"Well actually he told me all that yesterday, but I did have to be quiet and pay attention. In Los Angeles everybody wants to tell you their life's story. It's up to you whether you want to listen or not." All the creases in his ancient face smiled in unison.

I laughed knowingly, which made the old man's eyes light up. "Now that is funny. You meant it to be funny didn't you sir? Are you down here every morning doing your Tai Chi at sunrise?"

He nodded yes. "One must take advantage of every day you are blessed with. It is pleasing to see you laugh through your sorrow young man."

"I suppose you also knew laughter is what I do for a living?" I queried.

"No, but if you are able to impart the joy laughter you have been truly sanctified."

Despite the cleansing effect of the ocean's cool breeze and the old man's wisdom, I did not feel blessed. I acknowledged, "Your are right. I remember some nights when little else was going right; still I was still able to make some people laugh. It doesn't matter much now without Erin in my life."

His wizened eyes looked intensely into mine. "If she means that much to you, trust your heart. You will find a way back to her."

"Thanks for the tip sir; but it would be just like my heart to acquire this wisdom and then not let me know exactly what to do with it," I replied.

The old man spoke sagaciously. "Your do have the gift of humor. Please remember that laughter is much like love. It is but a moment long. However, a life without love or laughter is an ache that will endure forever."

I scarcely had time to absorb this wonderful old man's last prophecy, when we both heard a cry for help down by the ocean. Instinctively I ran down to see if I could lend a hand. I spotted that lawyer in the business suit bobbing up and down in the surf. So I ripped off my clothes and dove into the ocean after him. He seemed to be out of breath, as he was almost in my grasp. Desperately I lunged at him. I barely got a fist full of his suit jacket. He was way too weak to fend me off, so I was able to cross-chest carry him back to shore. When I dragged him up onto the beach his pallor was color of the morning sky.

The old man was standing over him. "Taking the preciousness of one's own life is a gesture that only serves to hurt the people who you leave behind."

"You are absolutely right sir. I had two suicides in my own family. That's why I'm not going to let this guy die damnit." Then I unbuttoned the lawyer's collar and gave him mouth-to-mouth resuscitation.

After what seemed like an eternity the lawyer started to spit up some water, and then gasped for air. The first words coughed out of his New York mouth were, "What the hell are you doing to me? Get your mouth off me you faggot? You had better back up off me right now butt puppet or I'm going to sue your ass for sexual harassment."

I was bowled over. "Sue me? The joke is on you buddy. I'm a comedian. I don't have any money. And, if I were gay I would have used a lot more tongue."

The old man smiled at me. "Sometimes the comforting thought of death can be deceiving, but any day above ground is worth celebrating."

The irascible New Yorker sputtered, "Who the fuck is this old Chinese schmuck? Oh yeah, I told yesterday where he could stick his stupid philosophy."

As I was putting my shirt back on, a yellow emergency lifeguard vehicle pulled up next to us.

I was approached by one of the lifeguards. He told me he could take over from here. Since my unappreciated job was finished, the old man and I wandered off together into the mist of the morning. "Some people are too foolish to realize when they have been given a second chance at life. That is why we must rejoice for him. I will show you how to release your inner power." With this said, the old man returned to his Tai Chi ritual. I attempted to follow his fluid movements without appearing too dorky.

Meanwhile back at Peggy's she was leaving for work. She frowned at Travis. "I am worried. Jordan hasn't slept in his bed all night and I don't have a clue where he is. He had a huge lover's quarrel last night, and Erin tossed him out with the trash. Travis do you have any idea where Jordan goes when he gets really depressed?"

Travis thought for a moment and yawned. "Wait a minute. Whenever he'd get bummed we would fire up a big fatty, and we'd drive to his favorite beach in Santa Monica. But, you said his car was still here."

Peggy grabbed her briefcase. "Well one of us has to a job to go to Travis. So you have to look for him. Here take my cell phone and call me when you find him. Come on get out of bed. Love you Travis. Bye."

Travis rolled his eyes in disbelief that he was up at 6:00 AM. He angrily muttered, "Thanks a heap Jordan. You could have done this at a decent hour, but no that would be thoughtful." He grabbed a cold cup of coffee, threw on some clothes, and wearily headed out the front door for the beach.

When Travis arrived at Santa Monica beach his eyes were wide with amazement at how many people were awake and active at this hour. He screamed with all the windows rolled up in his van. "It's too early you pin heads! Go back to your homes and take a damn nap! I wish I could, but noooo. I've got find Jordan before he gets run over by a yuppie asshole on skates or some dip wad on a bike."

Travis continued to mumble under his breath like a mental patient. He exited his van and grudgingly trudged down the Strand bike path looking for his buddy. A bicyclist and two skaters almost collided with Travis. They cursed at him. Travis screamed back, "I thought you morons worked out so you wouldn't be stressed out."

He looked toward the ocean as if for some relief. Travis was not pleased when he spotted me with the old Tai Chi master. Now a small group of us were doing these graceful martial arts exercises. Travis stalked down the beach to our group.

The old man acknowledged Travis. "Ah another member for our morning meditation?"

I could tell by the look on Travis's face that he was in not exactly in the mood for exercise. He was never in the mood for exercise. I had to ask him, "What are you doing here?"

Travis sarcastically replied, "I love the smell of Tai Chi in the morning. This shit is unbelievable Jordan. Peggy and I are worried crazy. So she made me look all over LA for you. And, what are you doing?

Chilling at the beach with this Tai Chi dude. Well you can walk the hell home? I'm out of here."

I stopped doing my exercises, stepped away from the group, and implored, "Hold on Travis. Come back here. Let's talk about this."

Now Travis was really worked up. "You think you are the only one in a jacked up relationship right now? I have zero privacy. Peggy's got my ass glued to this damn cell phone 24-7. She even walks in when I'm squatting on the crapper. What's next a Satellite Tracking System strapped to my ass? I can't go nowhere by myself. She makes me go shopping everywhere with her. Then I have to sit on that looser bench in the middle of the mall clutching her damn purse like a big fag. Jordan you've gotta help me. I'm so desperate I want to take up skydiving or bungee jumping, just for a shot in the hospital. Is it too early in the marriage to fake my own death?"

I was amazed. "This is unbelievable Travis. I thought you guys were doing great. Sure you both rushed into this marriage thing a bit quickly, but I assumed that was what you wanted?"

Travis quickly became even more animated. "Me too. Sure I was sick of having sex by lonesome all the time, but now I miss my freedom. I screwed up big time. She's your best friend Jordan. For the love of God help me."

"She may be my best friend, but now she's your wife Travis. It's up to you to let her know how you feel."

"Tell her how I feel? Nope I can't do that. That's a very bad idea," insisted Travis.

Concurrently Peggy and Erin were having a very different conversation on the phone. Peggy confided, "I will admit Erin I have gone with my share of jerks, but Travis is the nicest guy I've ever been with. I absolutely love that we go everywhere together."

"I love Jordan too, but he is terrified of marriage. I can't help feeling he only wants to see me if it's convenient, or if he is y."

"Even if that was true Erin you were still pretty tough on him. His bed wasn't slept in at all last night."

Erin's concern was evident in her tone. "I am really worried about him. It doesn't mean I want to see him right now, but do you have any idea where he went?"

"Travis thinks Jordan is at the beach somewhere. He has my cell phone. Let's conference-call him?"

Erin insisted, "Don't tell him I'm on the other line. It is way too soon for Jordan to think I've forgiven him."

Peggy dialed Travis at the beach. Travis twitched when he heard his cell phone ring. "Oh damn its Peggy. What am I going say?"

I hurriedly instructed him. "Whatever you do don't tell her I am down at the beach doing Tai Chi. She won't think I've suffered enough. Women love to feel like you are agonizing over your own stupidity."

Travis cautiously answered the phone. "Hello sugar babe. Yeah I found him. He was moping along the beach all by his lonesome."

I whispered loudly, "Tell her I saved a guy from drowning. It will make me look like I'm putting my life in danger."

Travis gave me a quizzical look and shrugged. Then he told Peggy, "Yeah Jordan even saved some guy from drowning. He's soaked to the bone."

I whispered loudly, "Did Peggy speak with Erin yet?"

"Jordan wants to know if you talked to Erin?"

Peggy lied. "She hasn't been in all morning. Glad you found Jordan. Boss is coming. Got to run."

Peggy waited for Travis to hang up. Afterward she asked Erin, "While they are at the beach let us get something to eat."

Peggy met Erin for lunch at an upscale Beverly Hills bistro. Erin began the conversation with, "Since you are so happy with married life I was wondering if you would help me out with Jordan?"

Peggy raised one eyebrow and questioned her motives. "Let me get this straight. You want me to figure out a way to trick my best friend into marrying you?"

Erin smiled sweetly and cajoled, "Peggy I am not asking you to help me trap him. You are the most intelligent person Jordan knows, and you do understand him better than anybody else."

Peggy's demeanor softened in the face of flattery. "Well you do have a point, and Jordan could certainly use some stability in his life."

Erin tried to hide her glee. "Good then you will help me out?"

Peggy capitulated. "It is for his own good. So I suppose so. What's your plan?"

In the interim at Peggy's condo Travis was hatching out a scheme of his own. First he questioned me. "Jordan you're my best bud? Right?"

"Sure I guess so. Why?"

Travis had calmed down a little from the beach, but he was still unrelenting. "Because, you gotta help me get away from Peggy. Sure there'll be some white lies, but it'll sound better coming out of you."

I was shocked and chagrined. "You've got to be kidding? She is my best friend in the world. She took me in right after my divorce when I was a financial and emotional wreck. Besides it would break her heart Travis."

Now Travis was becoming more agitated. "Oh yeah. Better to break my balls than her heart?"

"Right now I think Peggy's heart is a lot more delicate than your testicles. Sorry Travis,"

Travis exploded irrationally. "That's great! Take the woman's side like a big fag. Hell even sissies are more loyal to men than you."

"Of course gay guys are more loyal to men. They want other men you moron. I can't figure why you Texans are so snooty about homosexuals anyway. You shop at the same damn stores."

Travis was livid. "Oh now I'm a queer and a moron you two-faced ass wipe?"

Now I was getting pissed too. "No, because that would be an insult to actual gay morons everywhere." Travis screamed vitriolically. "Fuck you! Get the hell out of here Jordan! If your not gonna help me pack your shit and get out of this condo now."

Even though I was fuming I tried to be logical. "I hate to point this out, but this is Peggy's condo not yours; and you are the one who wants an annulment."

Travis stalked towards the front door and shouted, "Fine, because I want to be as far away from both you assholes as I can be."

"Travis you're broke. Where are you are going to live?"

Travis flung open the door and screamed, "I'll live in my damn van if I have to."

"Oh that's perfect Travis. Now you'll be homeless moron too."

Travis threw Peggy's cell phone at me. "Take this. From here on out you take her damn calls." Then he fumed out and slammed the door behind him.

I sat staring at the freshly slammed door in disbelief. Travis had gotten his wish after all. He had left me to be the bearer of his bad news. This was clearly not good. What was I going do? Should I tell Peggy the truth, use diplomacy, or fake a debilitating injury?

What a miserable turn of events. Now all of us were out in the relationship cold. Somehow I suspected that my problem was not the one that would receive the attention. With that thought in mind, I fell in to a deep sleep on the living room couch.

When Peggy came home she slammed the front door so hard that I sat bolt upright on the couch. I should have realized that Peggy had a rotten day at work. Unfortunately I was half asleep and not psychic.

So when she walked in the room I mumbled, "How was your day Peggy?"

I could tell I was in big trouble when she answered tersely, "I don't want to talk about it. Where's Travis? I have to talk to him right now."

I hoped to avoid revealing my fight with Travis. So I shrugged and told her, "I guess he's out?"

Peggy spotted her cell phone sitting on the table. Then she pressed me further. "I know that, but out where? He didn't take my cell phone."

I would have done anything to escape out that front door, so I told her, "I'd love to stay and chat, but I have pick up a check at the comedy club. If I run into Travis I'll tell him you are looking for him. Got to go. Bye"

Peggy stopped me in dead my tracks. "You know I can always tell when you are keeping something from me, and I want to know what it is. Sit down Jordan. We are going to talk about this right now."

Peggy possessed a bullshit detector like no other woman I had ever met. So I condescended. "All right you got me. Travis and I had a blow out, and he took off in his van. Now can I go?" I got up again to leave.

"No. Sit back down. I want to know exactly what this fight was about." She said obstinately.

"I think you need to talk to Travis about that." Peggy's infamous temper was close to blowing. "Then it was about me wasn't it? What did you do Jordan poison his brain with one of your stupid marital phobic tirades?"

I pleaded, "Peggy you are blaming the messenger. It was not my fault. Believe me I am on your side. I am always on your side."

"You know how many things I've done for you Jordan? But, if you don't want to tell me about Travis, oh I guess that's all right." Peggy's harried tone was beginning to guilt me.

I knew if I told her exactly how Travis felt it would somehow become my fault. So had to think fast. "I'm aware I owe you a lot Peggy. I also know that it was you who sent Travis to the beach after me. So I will return the favor and find him for you. Then we can all have a heart to heart?"

Peggy relented. "All right just find him and bring him back here. It had better be before I have to go to bed or I won't be able to sleep."

I realized that I had just scarcely side stepped the full force of hurricane Peggy. So I vowed to her in my best Richard Burton voice. "Your truculent Texan will be returned to you forthwith me lady." Then I immediately fled out the front door to Barry's comedy club before she could change her mind.

The minute I pulled up in front of The Comedy Club I spotted Travis's van. When I exited my car I realized that there is nothing like being immersed in someone else's problems to make you almost forget your own.

When I entered the club I became aware of Travis sneaking a look at me. I stole a look back at him. Now we were both acting like a couple kids. So I went over to confront him, but Travis spoke first. "What the hell are you doing here?"

"I just couldn't live another second without your sunny disposition Travis," I countered sarcastically.

"Bite me Jordan," he snapped.

"That's clever. You should try it on a heckler."

"Look asshole you got something to say to me spit it out," Travis snarled.

I thought for a minute then spoke. "All right. I think you have to stop running away from how you feel all the time, and go back and talk this out with Peggy. You owe her that much."

Before either of us could utter another word a sultry waitresses named Brandy strutted over to Travis and put her arm around him. She breathed sensually in his ear, "You promised we could go out to eat Travis. I'm ready now."

I couldn't resist saying, "You certainly are Brandy. Well Travis it seems I've underestimated you again. You should have made the perfect husband. Weasels mate for life don't they?"

Brandy looked mystified. "What does he mean by that Travis?"

"I don't even think he knows. Let's split Brandy," Travis hedged. Then he made a move for the door.

Now it was my turn to blow up. "Look you shallow self absorbed jack off. You are not going anywhere except back to Peggy's condo. Then you can explain to her why you are treating her like shit lately. I'm sorry Brandy, but Travis is married to my best friend. You are only a convenient pit stop that allows him to overlook that right now. If you want to be treated like some disposable bimbo, you'll have to stand in line behind his wife Peggy."

Brandy lashed out at an embarrassed Travis. "Is that true Travis? Are you really married? Damn you! Damn you to hell! Men are such dogs."

"Not really. Dogs are faithful, and will do anything for you if you feed them regularly."

That last line got to Travis, and made Brandy slink off in a huff. It sure did not stop her from picking up another comic on her way to the back bar.

Travis glared at me and scoffed, "Thanks a whole bunch Jordan."

"Please Travis. I probably saved you from a really nasty social disease. Now let's get your uninfected ass out of here right now."

Travis knew how persistent I could be so he relented. "I know you ain't about to leave me alone. So let's do it." We headed for the exit together.

Brandy was already playing tongue hockey with her latest conquest before we even reached the door.

On the way to our cars Travis implored, "You're not going to tell Peggy about Brandy are you?"

"Why would I do that? You were just going out for a bite weren't you?" I scoffed with a smirk.

We arrived at Peggy's she was getting ready for bed. She smiled warmly at me. "You always were good about keeping your word Jordan. Thanks." When Peggy noticed I was not leaving she added, "Don't you have go to the store for something?"

I feigned agreement. "Oh, yeah I have to pick up some uh, toilet paper. Talk to you guys later."

I exited the condo, but something held me there in the hallway. Maybe it was the sound of Peggy's voice booming through the thick front door. She was never one to hold back her emotions.

She screamed, "Travis can you tell me why you took off when you knew I was coming right home? You didn't even take my cell phone. You had to know that I wanted to talk to you about Jordan and Erin, not to mention this distant feeling I've been getting from you lately."

Being able to listen in on something I was bound to hear two different versions of later fascinated me somehow. Initially all Travis could do was stammer, "I, I didn't know you wanted to talk to me about Erin and Jordan. About this distant thing, I don't know what you're getting at sugar babe."

I knew how reprehensible eavesdropping was and yet I could not pull my ear away from our front door. I overheard Peggy carry on at top volume. "You had to know I wanted to talk about their fight? I was the one who sent you to the beach after him. And you know exactly what I'm mean by your being aloof lately. We haven't talked or cuddled after making love since we got back from our honeymoon in Vegas."

I was really glad I was on this side of the door. I only hoped no one would catch me eavesdropping. All Travis could do was to try to deny any culpability. His defense was, "I figured we would talk about Jordan when I got back. You are right about the not talking after sex thing, but I ain't been distant. I married you, I moved in, and I have been in touch with you every second of every day."

Now Peggy sounded hurt. "You make like closeness sound is a chore. Is that what I am to you Travis, a chore?"

I thought, man has she got him now. How is he going to talk his way out of this one? He tried. "Peggy I love being with you and talking and all, but I like bein' with my buddies too. You understand don't you baby?"

Travis must have gone over to hug her. Peggy yelled, "Don't touch me!" I heard someone stumble across the floor followed by Peggy screaming, "If you want to be with your friends so much, why don't you just leave now?"

Travis yelled, "You punched me!"

"It was a shove you big baby."

I heard Travis start for the front door so I immediately backed away and dashed down the hallway towards the elevator. Then I snuck into the stairwell next to it. I didn't hear any more footsteps so I peeked down the hallway towards our front door.

When I didn't see anybody I crept back down the hall and paused at our door. All I heard were the sounds of Peggy saying, "I'm sorry I didn't mean to push you so hard Travis."

Travis tones were soft and conciliatory too. "Well it hurt. I am sorry about this too sugar. This whole marriage thing is real new to both of us."

What did I miss? How could they have gone from combat to making up in a matter of seconds? Peggy's next words gave me a clue. "The reason I'm so clingy was because I was afraid of loosing you. I know I probably went a little too far with the cell phone, and walking in on you in the bathroom and all."

Travis pressed his position. "Do you swear not to barge into the bathroom any more, particularly when I'm on the can? A man needs his privacy."

"As long as you promise not to disappear without calling when I expect you to be home for dinner. It makes me worry about you."

Travis conceded. "I think you got yourself a deal little lady." I could tell by the moaning and groaning that followed that the verbal part of their making up had just come to an end.

As I snuck away from our front door I thought, damn Travis was actually truthful with her, and Peggy let him know exactly how she felt. Why this could easily work for Erin and me. All right not easily, but honesty was worth a shot wasn't it? Who was I kidding? I never believed I was going to be any good at marriage in the first place. How could I now inflict my inadequacies on yet another person whom I love?

Then I passed the condo next to ours and overheard a young couple fornicating at top volume.

I assumed they were young or they'd be dead by now. Their lusty lovemaking tested the limits of human endurance as far as I was concerned. Not that I wanted to listen to them, I had to.

Then it hit me that I not just eavesdropped once, but twice. This was something I despised; and what's worse, I had gained nothing from it at all.

I didn't think I was quite ready to speak with Erin. However, I did feel just miserable enough to go back to The Comedy Club and tell some jokes.

On my way out of our building a small fluffy white Poodle ran up to me. I bent down to pat him, and he started humping my leg. I tried to shake him off, but he was a persistent little -doggie.

Then I spotted my car and there was a tattooed, body pierced gay couple leaning against it.

To my complete mortification they began to passionately French kiss. Even when I inserted my key in the car door they wouldn't stop. I eased inside my beat up rice burner and started the engine. These two guys were still in a terminal tongue lock. I didn't want to honk the because, well that would've been rude. So I leaned out my car window and implored, "Uh excuse me gentlemen. Hello! I hate to interrupt, but I really must be going."

It was only then that they attempted to part lips, but couldn't. It seems their tongue studs were locked together. I asked them, "Should I dial 911 and request the Jaws of Life?" They shook their heads no in unison. The tattooed duo then hopped blissfully away into night with their tongues still locked together. I quietly pulled out of the parking space. As much as I hated witnessing the personal pain of others, this one did put a smile on my face on the way to Barry's comedy club. All I could think of was the sexual sounds I'd over heard at our condo complex, not to mention my erotic thoughts of Erin. My ardor was quickly quelled by the thought of the tongue stud boys, who were undoubtedly still stuck together.

When I entered The Comedy Club a strange bug-eyed man collared me. He began zealously lecturing me on the virtues of Scientology, and then rudely shoved some pamphlets in my face. I politely told him, "No thank you. I already have a personality."

I quickly sprinted into the safety of The Comedy Club. Owner Barry took notice and waved me over to his table. He leaned into me and whispered, "I just had a comic cancel on me Jordan. Do you want to go on next?"

"Sure Barry thanks." Barry gave the rap it up sign to the MC on stage, and pointed to me. When the MC announced my name I rushed on stage. As I did a well-built woman in a skintight tube top stood up. I was then forced to ask, "How many men here would like to back pack through her cleavage? Why is it that women in skin-tight clothes get leered at, while men in Speedos get laughed at? Why is masturbation is called self-abuse and boxing is a respected sport? Smacking the salami is only self-abuse if your mom or wife catches you isn't it? Do you think its possible to be sexually harassed on the set of a porno film? Is a bisexual just a gay person who is afraid to commit, or a greedy bastard who wants a shot at everybody? And, if your wife ever asks you do you think she is pretty, should you just grab a beer and head for the door? You know you can't win. Then she tells you she knows that woman had a boob and a nose job. Why tell us? Men don't care if a woman's entire body has more plastic than a Corvette. We still want to look. No. We have to look. We don't know how women can checkout a guy's butt with only a click of the eyeballs? Men can't do that. She'll say if you loved me you wouldn't look at other women. I said if you loved **me** you'd let me look at other women, and if you **really** loved me you'd let me bring them home for a 3-way? If she continues to berate you for looking at other women, just start looking at other guys. (Lisp) Aren't his pecks and thighs just fabulous honey? Why is the Catholic Church is against homosexuality? Sure it would thin out the priesthood. Who does the Pope think made his robe and hat? (Lisp) Let's put gold and jewels over this cape Miss Thing. The pontiff will look absolutely stunning. Hell if I knew how to dress better I would be gay. Instead I dress like I have been jumped by a Goodwill box. Tonight I am so confused I feel like a lesbian trapped in a man's body. My ex asked me do you know why we didn't have any children, because you were shooting blanks? I told her it would've helped if I had a moving target. I should have known it wouldn't work out from the start. During the wedding ceremony she was hitting on one of the bridesmaids. As we walked down the isle they played "Love Stinks" and "Highway to Hell". Instead of you may kiss the bride the priest announced, 'All right let's get ready to rumble!'" The laughter convinced me that, unlike Erin, the crowd was mine.

I contend, "You have to keep trying don't you? At the beach yesterday I saw a gorgeous woman in a see through thong bikini. She looked directly at me and told me that my eyes matched my swimming trunks. I replied, 'Why? Are they bulging too?'"

"Then she beat the crap out of me, so I followed her home. From religion to relationships we embrace unnecessary pain. Our current fascination for body piercing and tattoos proves that people can't get enough pain. A pierced penis is popular now. Personally you couldn't pay me enough cash to slap my joystick on a table, and tell some drug-fueled ex-biker to go ahead and pound a metal spike right on through that bad boy."

I had this crowd on such a roll that their laughter was like sexual heat steaming off a woman's body. They applauded for more. "Tonight I saw this kid on Hollywood Blvd. He had six earrings, with a chain connected to a nipple ring and a nose ring. I pulled the chain and it flushed his head. What if a body-studded couple got divorced? Who gets custody of the nipple-rings? I did discover that nipple rings are a good place to hang your spare car keys during sex."

One guy in the audience was bent over laughing. So I pointed at him and indicated, "Does your mom ever call when you are having sex sir? Mine does. I'm an idiot, so I answered the phone. "Oh, oh, oooooh! OH YEESSS! Oh hi mom? I'm out of breath from jogging. OOOOH GOD **YES!** It's just a foot cramp mom. Dinner after church with the family? Sure, sure I'll be there. Ooooh YES, YES, YES! You are the best! Mom. See you on Sunday. Bye." The laughter, applause and my monologue reached climax at the same time; so I bowed deeply and exited the stage.

What I failed to notice was Barry furtively turning off his tape recorder. Then he surreptitiously slipped it under the table into his jacket pocket. When I approached his table he took that same hand out of his pocket and shook mine with a smile on his face. He enthused, "Nice set Jordan. You did some new stuff. Pretty funny. Have to talk to you later. I've got to take a meeting in my office right now." When Barry departed all that lingered was a trail of his stale cigar smoke.

I didn't quite know how to construe what Barry had just told me, so I left the club. I only hoped Peggy and Travis would take their sex-capades into her bedroom by the time I got home.

Back up in Barry's office he was in a meeting all right, with Harvey and Bob. Unbeknownst to Travis or me, Bob and Harvey had hustled the rough draft of our script over to their studio bosses. We never did find out what their superiors appreciated least, our unedited script or the alcohol wafting from Bob's breath. At any rate both of them eventually got called on the carpet and promptly canned. Now they were independent of any studio ethics. So Bob and Harvey decided to disappear and take whatever scripts they could abscond with. At this point they seemed intent on dragging Barry into their little covert coven of craven chicanery.

Even after a killer gig like tonight's I felt a little depressed. I figured why not take a chance on furthering this feeling with a swing by Erin's?

When I arrived at Erin's I noticed a bright red Ferrari parked in her driveway. It couldn't possibly belong to her ex-boyfriend Earl. Slowly my curiosity got the best of me. As a result I waited hunched down in my car like a private dick on a stake out.

I must have dozed off, because the next thing I heard was her front door close, and the unmistakable roar of a Ferrari starting up. As the car drove by, I sat up and recognized the same guy in the three-piece suit who had been at the restaurant with Erin. Should I confront her with this, or just drive home and hope that the fluffy Poodle will try to hump my leg again? I opted for the small dog, because at least I knew what to expect from him.

When I arrived home in my mortification-mobile, what was left of my self-esteem had hit rock bottom.

I realized that Erin was now with a guy who could do more for her than I ever could. Bob and Harvey weren't returning my calls, and I was perilously close to flat broke.

Could my father have been right? Perhaps I was a waste of skin. Even when I passed the homeless guy outside our condo complex I thought at least he's got no ballooning credit card bills and no overhead. Boy was I wallowing knee deep in my own miasma. Then I figured, things could be worse. After all I did have my health. Just then I sneezed and my back went out.

Slowly and painfully I dragged myself into the elevator then pushed the up button. I limped to our condo. With my luck I maybe Travis and Peggy were rutting around on the floor like a couple of wart hogs in heat. OK now I was hoping they were, because I could've used the entertainment value.

Instead when I walked in, I tripped over one of Peggy's cats and went sprawling on the floor in a spasm of abject pain and frustration. The cat yowled and scurried under the couch where it spent most of its life anyway. Peggy and Travis came running out of their bedroom and yelled, "What happened Jordan? Are you all right?" I was sprawled on my back like a helpless turtle unable to get up. They bent over and assisted me to my feet. Both assured me, "We were really worried about you when you didn't come home."

As they helped ease my aching body onto the couch I teased, "Oh yeah, you were in such deep concern you probably didn't even realize I was gone. When I walked out of here the tension was thick enough to cut up and serve with pasta. I was just glad neither of you had a gun. By the way how did that loud discussion turn out?"

"We talked and uh. Well you know." Travis volunteered.

Peggy grinned. "We kissed and made up. Didn't we sweetheart?"

"We couldn't sleep. That damn couple next door was knocking boots at top volume," yawned Travis.

"Yet another couple that's having more fun than I am. Too bad I never met them. Maybe I could suggest a framage-a-trois. Yes a three way with cheese would be nice. I'm that lonely."

Peggy shook her head in disbelief. You men are perverts you know that?"

"And we love that about ourselves," I interjected.

Travis reminded her, "Wait a darn minute sweetheart, you married a man remember? By the way Jordan you didn't wander down to the club and run into Harvey or Bob did you?"

"I went down to the club, but I didn't see either of them. I had a killer set, but Barry was acting really weird like he was trying to hide something,"

"He wasn't acting Jordan. Barry is weird. I don't trust his ass at all." Travis scowled.

"Of course you don't trust him Travis. He is a nightclub owner,"

"Why don't we both go to the club and ask Barry if Harvey or Bob have been around," questioned Travis.

"Like you are going to get a straight answer out of him. Barry is so sleazy the only reason he'd ever go to confession is to talk dirty to a priest."

"We just got to ask the other comics then," Travis suggested.

"Terrific idea. When ever you want the straight poop talk to the competition," I added sarcastically. "We don't got a choice."

Peggy yawned loudly. "As stimulating as this is guys, I think I'm going to bed. Some of us have to work for a living. Travis are you coming?" She drowsily trundled off to bed.

"Sure baby be right there," he assured her. Then he turned to me and whispered, "I can tell something else is bugging you Jordan but it's gonna have to wait."

I assured him. "Travis it's just my back. It's completely out. Please help me into bed." I was way too embarrassed to reveal what my snooping on Erin had revealed.

Meanwhile back at Erin's the well-dressed man with the Ferrari sat on her living room couch oozing charm from every pore. Erin, on the other hand, was all business. She proceeded to pour over his legal briefs, while he only pressed to move closer to her on the couch. Erin kept sliding over until she bumped into the armrest. She removed her glasses and looked sternly into his eyes. "Please Madison I can't deal with these divorce papers and fend you off at the same time. I appreciate your bringing over the Chinese food, but we have got a lot of work to do here. It seems your wife wants her share of the community property and yours."

Madison persistently tried to remove the legal papers from Erin's lap. He cajoled, "Erin you know I'm crazy about you. We're not going to court for a couple of weeks. Let's relax for a while. Here have a glass of Merlot."

Erin smiled. "Madison I am flattered, but you know me better than to mix business with pleasure. Besides you are still legally married and I'm in love with somebody else."

Madison smoothly stated, "I really don't believe you are still in love with that comic. Even so it certainly doesn't preclude us getting together."

Erin let out an audible sigh. "It never ceases to amaze me the way a man can so completely divorce his sex urge from his actual brain."

Madison continued to inveigle. "Is that a yes we can or a no we can't Erin?"

The following morning I couldn't determine which was worse, my emotional pain or the one in my back. Fortunately I had a chiropractor friend named Dr. John who would adjust my back for free.

The catch was that I had to listen to his apocalyptic tirades about coming of the rapture. I told him that I knew the end of civilization was near, when I found out the top selling Rap artist was white. As a man who used to be white I was personally offended. It should not have surprised me that his back adjustment that day was more painful than usual. You have to appreciate a man who enjoys his work. Dr. John also told me I needed more exercise, and that it would probably improve my sex life. He was right.

The next day I went to Gold's Gym, and two burly body builders tried to clean and jerk me. I was so desperate I would have settled for a jerk and clean. They also suggested some abdominal squat thrusts. Squatting around them? Let me rub down the goose bumps. I even lied to them, about being bisexual so they wouldn't bother me. I explained this was my day for women, and then split for my car. I suppose one of the advantages to being bisexual is that you can be propositioned by men, and yet still rejected by women. I know that feeling.

There was only one woman I was being rejected by right now, but not unlike Bob and Harvey, Erin wouldn't return my calls either. This has got to be a pandemic problem in L.A. People in this town have a myriad of beepers, voice mail, e-mail, call forwarding, and a cell phone surgically implanted in their face; and yet no one will even fax me the finger. I'll bet big time Steven Spielberg and Jack Nicholson never have this problem.

I finally decided I had to call their studio's head office, and see if they'd seen either Bob or Harvey. When I finally got through to the executive secretary she told me they had been fired weeks ago. I asked about my movie script, she didn't know anything except when they cleared out their office they took everything with them. I immediately rushed home to tell Travis and Peggy.

When I arrived at our condo I asked Peggy where Travis was? Peggy greeted me with, "Travis is out looking for a real job Jordan. What are you going to do about rent this month?" I knew at once I could forget about her lending an understanding ear to any of my problems, but I told her about them anyway.

Peggy advised me, "You had better locate those Bob and Harvey flakes real soon. It sounds to me like they are trying to rip you off."

Once again Peggy astounded me with her grasp of the obvious. I couldn't help shaking that feeling that club owner Barry was concealing something too. I needed Travis for a diversionary tactic, and I was too antsy to sit at home and wait for him. So I asked Peggy, "Where do you think Travis went looking for work?"

"You are going to drag him back down to that stupid comedy club again aren't you?"

I didn't want to lie to my best friend. Peggy knew me all too well, so I had better sound sincere. "I wouldn't do that to you Peggy. I was thinking maybe Travis knows where I could get a job too. We might even be able to work in the same place."

Peggy offered, "Travis's last real job was as an orderly at an insane asylum. He had to quit there when the patients started beating him at poker." I thanked her and then left with the employment section of the LA Times tucked under my arm. Travis had circled a couple of hospital help wanted ads.

I finally tracked down Travis at an LA county mental institution. Travis told me that working inside this place was just like being a patient there. It was just my luck that they needed another warm body to help out. So I let them hire me.

I figured it couldn't be any more bizarre than being brought up in the dementia of my own family. Boy was I wrong. This facility made "The Cuckoo's Nest" look like a Kathy Lee Gifford Carnival Cruise. Travis and I worked in separate wings of the facility. His patients seemed to have much more severe disorders than mine.

I soon learned that most of the patients in my section were neither a danger to themselves nor anyone else. Most of my patients were attempting to escape people or situations they were unable to handle on their own. One particular man named Warner chose to open up to me. He confessed, "I committed myself just to get away from my petulant parents and a wife whose favorite indoor hobby was nagging me incessantly."

"Let me get this straight. You're locked up in here twenty-four hours a day only to get away from your ill tempered relatives? Don't you miss your freedom?"

Warner admitted, "In here I have freedom, from my family. Oh that's right you haven't met them as yet."

Warner continued, "My relatives will be here on Sunday. It's visiting day. Do not even try to find me. My wife labored under the delusion that she could berate me into loving her, or pester me into an erection. Sorry that was probably a little more than you wanted to know wasn't it?"

Are you kidding me that was more than anyone needed to know? I guess talking to Warner about the virtues of family values was out of the question. I half understood how he felt, because my own father was distant and abusive. However, my mother was, and will always be the brightest beacon of light shinning in my life. When all else failed to cheer her up, she would invariably call me in California to make her laugh. I never let her down. I would have tried to find out if Warner had someone like my mother in his life, but he seemed more intent on isolation from his family than any introspection.

Most of the other patients were even more withdrawn. This was especially true of one particular old redheaded woman. She was always huddled in the corner of the TV room away from everyone. I'm not sure why, but I was inexorably drawn to her. Perhaps it was the fact that I was a sucker for women in distress, especially if they had red hair.

I asked Warner about the reclusive woman in the corner. He divulged, "She was such an out of control drunk and drug addict that not even AA wanted her."

I realized that culling additional information from the doctors about her would probably make them think I was infringing on their turf. This hospital staff seemed much more interested in medicating the patients than finding out the real root of their problems. A thick medicinal stench lingered in the hospital's air like a foreboding blanket of tulle fog. This haze of hopelessness seemed to pervade the psyches of most of the patients as well.

Getting through this drug-induced stupor to reach this reclusive redhead would not be easy. My first ploy was to find out what she liked. Warner told me the only time he ever saw her smile was when someone had given her a piece of strawberry cheesecake.

The following day I decided to sneak some cheesecake into the hospital. When I first approached the huddled woman she recoiled. Then I showed her a piece of strawberry cheesecake. She brushed the tangled red hair away from her sad face. I saw her pale blue eyes brightened just a little. I cautiously offered her the cheesecake. She snatched it out of my hand in one quick motion and instantly devoured it. Then she looked at me innocently with a slight smile creeping across her weathered face. I was sure I heard her whisper, "Thank you."

I responded hesitantly, "You're welcome. I'm sorry I don't know your name."

For no reason she started singing and swaying at the same time. "My name is McNamara I'm the leader of the band." The rest of the words were somewhat incoherent, because she didn't seem to know just what they were. She continued to sing them anyway. "My name is McNamara I'm the leader of the band."

When Warren had walked up to me. I whispered, "Why is she singing about McNamara's band?"

"Because, her name is McNamara that's why."
I couldn't help asking Warren, "Do you think she ever had any children, like daughter named Erin maybe?"

Evidentially Mrs. McNamara had heard me, because she abruptly stopped singing, and glowered menacingly at me. When she stood up and started towards me with a look of disdain on her on heavily lined face I retreated. Warren feebly stumbled towards an orderly. Then she me pushed against a wall and tears started flowing down her ashen cheeks. She reached out and clutched my shirt, and began to sob inconsolably on my shoulder.

One of the staff doctors rushed over and began to shout at me. "What the HELL do you think you are doing? Your job is not to upset the patients. Your job is to clean up after them. Now move away from Mrs. McNamara and get back to work. What are you waiting for? Move now you idiot!"

After the doctor had departed with Mrs. McNamara Warren skulked over to me. He reluctantly revealed,

"Jordan that was unbelievable. The doctors have been trying to achieve a break through like that with Mrs. McNamara ever since her arrival here."

"Yeah there must be something about me that really pisses redheads off. My girlfriend Erin can't stop yelling at me either."

"Do you think that your Erin is really Mrs. Me Namara's daughter? She never mentioned having a daughter, but then she never said much of anything."

"The way she reacted when I mentioned Erin's name indicates that it means something to her. The only problem is that my Erin told me her mother was dead. I have to determine for certain if that woman really is her mother."

Warren whispered, "You'd better not let Dr Mengale' find out, or he'll fire you so fast it will make your head spin."

I grinned. "Is that what you call that doctor who yelled at me? That's funny."

He confided, "I'm sure Dr. Mengale' wouldn't think so." After that Warren smiled back at me for the very first time.

It looked as if I had encountered yet another person here who was humor challenged. That could mean only one thing. My work here was not done.

I thought my biggest problem would be how to get Mrs. McNamara out of the earshot of Dr. Mengale', so I could ask her some pertinent questions. First I searched the entire institution, but couldn't find Mrs. McNamara anywhere. Finally I asked Warren where she was. He told me, "The doctors probably put her in isolation, and are reevaluating her medication."

"Why the hell would the doctors put a woman in isolation who has already chosen to put herself there?"

Warren shrugged, "I guess the staff doctors don't want any interference with their treatment policy."

"Of course not. They have done such a superb job on Mrs. McNamara so far."

Warren repressed a smile. "You're being cynical again aren't you Jordan?"

"Can't get a darn thing by you Warren. Now will you help me find out where Mrs. McNamara is? I have something I'm sure she will be very interested in."

Warren looked about furtively and whined, "I can't help you or they will put me in isolation too. Oh dear here comes one of them now." With that said, Warren whisked out of the TV area and down the hall to his own room.

My only other ally at the hospital was Travis, but if I got him in trouble Peggy would have my butt. This plan would take a Wiley Coyote like cunning.

Meanwhile back at Erin's place she and Madison hashed out the finer points of his case. Madison began with, "Come on you must have known from the very beginning that I was falling for you Erin."

"And, you must have known that I was not interested. I don't plan on being the next rebound babe in your little black Rolodex. So let's restrict ourselves to just discussing your wife's incompatibility lawsuit." Erin was insistent.

"Yeah, yeah I know. My wife's spending is incompatible with my income. Now why don't you like me Erin?"

"How about the fact that you are still legally married, and I'm your attorney. This working arrangement doesn't include any social contact."

Madison smiled and cooed, "But, it could."

"What between "n" and "o" don't you understand Madison?"

Madison breathed an exasperated sigh. "It's that Jordan guy isn't it? I still don't get how you can be hung up on some broke comedian who won't even ask you to marry him"

Erin glared back at him. "Is it love or just women that you don't understand Madison? I'm nothing like your soon to become ex-wife. Not all women are about money."

Madison attempted a different tact. "I know that. I also know I fell for you the moment our eyes first met. Sure my wife dumping me has made me more vulnerable, but is that such a bad thing? You of all people know what an inconsiderate lout I've been in the past. I am trying to change here. With you in my life Erin I know I can be a better man."

His pleas began to soften her a little. "Madison that is a beautiful sentiment, and I appreciate you as a friend and a legal colleague. However, you have to admit the timing is just not right. First let's see if we can get through this divorce with a shred of dignity, and some of your assets in tact."

Madison was obviously disappointed, yet remained persistent. "O.K. let's wrap up this legal mess, so we can get on to more important matters like us."

Back at the mental hospital I realized that I had to have Travis's help to locate Mrs. McNamara. I told him, "Look Travis I am certain this woman is Erin's mother, and these so-called doctors are keeping her drugged up and hidden away from everyone."

I was surprised by his answer. "Jordan them staff doctors got to know what they are doing.

Besides if we piss these dudes off they'll can us in a heart beat."

I implored him. "Come on Travis. These white coated clowns are keeping this woman a prisoner, and you don't even want to know why?"

"Look man I just work here and I can't afford to loose this gig right now. You can't either Jordan. We both owe Peggy a load of money."

I tried a sympathetic appeal. "I'm sure Erin would want to know if her mother were alive. Wouldn't you if it were your mom Travis? Please let's help her out, before these doctors destroy what few brain cells Mrs. McNamara has left."

"Erin's dad said that her mom was dead. There's a wagonload of red heads named McNamara's out there. That woman could be anybody," Travis stated emphatically.

I shook my head no. "Erin's father lied to her about a lot of things. You didn't see the way this woman reacted when she heard Erin's name, and the way she looked at me before she broke down and sobbed.

When you meet her you'll know she's Erin's mom. I'm begging you to help me."

Just then the doctor known as Mengale' strode resolutely by us and demanded, "You two are not getting paid to stand around and wag your tongues are you? Get your mops and buckets and clean out those bathrooms. What are you waiting for you idiots?"

Travis bristled at the doctor's calloused disrespect, but both of us moved quickly into the janitor's supply closet. When we closed the door Travis exploded, "That little sawed off turd! I would pound his face ugly, but God beat me to it."

Then I spotted a couple of white doctor's smocks in the supply closet, and a light went off in my head. "Travis look doctor's smocks. Someone has left us a perfect way to ferret out Mrs. McNamara. Here try this on. They fit well enough don't they? What do say we go find Erin's mother?"

Travis got a mischievous grin on his face and admitted, "I think I might know where she is. They make me clean every damn room in this place except one in the east wing. Let's go check it out."

We snuck out of the closet and down the hall towards the west wing. Other doctors were nodding at us like we were part of their staff. When we arrived at the west wing Travis whispered, "There's that room they won't let me in. Let's take a look see." We cautiously peered in through the small glass window on the door.

"There's Mrs. McNamara huddled over there in the corner." Travis quickly clasped his hand over my mouth, because two real doctors were coming up behind us.

One of the real doctors asked, "You two doctors are new here aren't you?"

"Yes. My name is Dr. Dre. We were sent down here to check up on Mrs. McNamara, but Dr. Wiley forgot his keys. You don't happen to have the key to this door here do you doctor?"

The doctor thought for a moment, then he opened the door. He reminded us, "Just let yourselves out when you are done. The door will lock itself when you leave."

Once inside the room Travis chided, "Why did you have to tell them my real name? You used a fake one." Then we crept into the isolation room.

"Sorry Travis those doctors caught me by surprise." When I looked over at Mrs. McNamara she recoiled at first. Slowly she tried to focus on our faces through her drugged induced fog. Next she nodded her weary head, and wiped drool off her mouth.

I was reluctant to do what I had planned, but this would probably be my only chance. I cautiously approached the dazed woman, and pulled an old picture from my pocket. She gazed up at me with a glimmer of recollection.

I gently inquired, "Hello Mrs. McNamara remember me? I'm the one who brought you the strawberry cheesecake. Take a look at this photograph. Do you recognize her? Is this your daughter?" I showed her a picture of Erin as a very young girl. Her bleary eyes widened with a shock of recognition. I turned to

Travis. "See I wasn't making this stuff up. It is her mother."

While my head was turned Mrs. McNamara jumped up, grabbed me by the lapels, and spat in my face. She started screaming, "You son of a bitch! What have you done with my daughter? So help me God I didn't want to leave her. My husband forced me to. That bastard beat me. He drove me away from my only child. Oh God I abandoned my own flesh and blood. I am totally worthless. Help me doctor. Please help me get out of here. I have to see her. Erin forgive me." Finally she let go of me and slowly sank to the floor sobbing hysterically.

I bent down on my knees and put my hands on the poor woman's shoulders. "She is not a little girl any more Mrs. McNamara. Now she is a beautiful young woman, and I am sure she wants to see you too."

Back at Erin's Madison plied her with a combination of charm, persistence, and wine to wear down her resistance. "Erin please don't think I am only attracted to you, because I'm on the rebound. My wife and I grew apart years ago. I can't even remember the last time we were intimate. Tonight I've tried to control my desire for you, but I can't any longer. You know I've always loved you Erin. Give us that chance we both deserve. You know in your heart we belong together." He kissed her, but she struggled to resist and pushed him away. Right now his passion wasn't the only thing that was on the rise.

Meanwhile back at the mental institution I asked Travis, "Check out that little window and see if anyone is coming. We have to get another doctor's gown out of that supply closet in order to sneak Mrs. McNamara out of this place."

Travis looked worried and shook his head no. "I just can't. We'll catch too much crap if we get caught Jordan."

I smiled. "Who said anything about getting caught. We'll simply slip Mrs. McNamara out of here and the doctors will assume she escaped. Don't worry it'll be a walk in the park."

"Sure it'll be a regular day at the beach. You know you are full of shit Jordan." Then he peeked out the little window on the isolation door. "You know why? Right now there are two real doctors headed straight down the hall for our door. What now Einstein?"

Suddenly Mrs. McNamara became surprisingly lucid. She instructed us, "Quick get into that little bathroom. I'll get rid of them if they come in here." We rushed into the bathroom. When the two doctors looked through the small window Mrs. McNamara pretended to lapse back into a withdrawn drugged state. When they went away she shouted, "The coast is clear. Let's get moving boys." We stuffed a bunch of towels under a blanket and placed it in the same corner Mrs. McNamara had huddle in.

We rushed out of the isolation room, and made our way to the utility closet. Mrs. McNamara was curious. "How did you figure out I was Erin's mother?"

"There is a family resemblance; but your reaction when I mentioned her name in the TV room was the clincher. Quick look drugged out Mrs. McNamara. Here come some real doctors again."

She feigned a drugged out stupor. Then one of the real doctors inquired, "Do you two need any assistance? Your patient looks pretty out of it."

I smiled and assured them, "We have to keep her that way. It's part of her treatment."

One of the doctors confided, "God knows what a mad house this place would be if all these patients weren't on drugs."

"Isn't that the truth?" I nodded in agreement.

They passed by us just as we arrived at the utility closet. We quickly whipped inside the supply room. I outfitted Mrs. McNamara with a doctor's smock. We fixed her hair. After that we bolted out of the hospital complex and into the parking lot.

Hurrying to Travis's van with a woman coming off sedatives was not easy. We all let out a shout of jubilation when Travis opened his van door.

Suddenly the door was slammed in our faces. An ominous voice demanded, "Exactly where do you lackeys think you're going with my patient? It was Dr. Mengale'. His foreboding tone froze us in our tracks.

Mrs. McNamara, on the other hand, looked Dr. Mengale' dead in the eye and declared, "We are going to go see my daughter and you can't stop us."

Dr. Mengale' assured us, "I can and I will. None of you are going anywhere. Now get back in that hospital before I call the police."

Mrs. McNamara nudged the doctor aside to get into Travis's van. Dr. Mengale' grabbed her from behind and dragged her to the ground. She scrambled to her feet with a look of sheer contempt on her face.

When the doctor cocked his fist Mrs. McNamara punched him right in the nose.

He fell to the ground clutching his face. Mengale' mumbled through his bloody hands, "You broke my nose you crazy old bitch. Mark my words all of you will pay for this."

As she got into the van Mrs. McNamara guaranteed him, "Not tonight we're not. Let's get going boys. Erin is waiting." When we drove off I only hoped those sirens in the distance were for not for us.

We then raced to Erin's place, and leaped out of Travis's van. I couldn't wait to see the look on Erin's face when I introduced her to her long lost mother.

I walked up and knocked on the front door. There was no answer, but her car was in the driveway. So I knocked again and the door swung open.

I immediately thought oh God I hope she's all right. Mrs. McNamara and Travis cautiously followed me into the darkened house. I heard rustling noises and moans so I called out, "Erin its Jordan. Are you all right sweetheart?" Without waiting for a reply I went over and switched the lights on.

There on the living room couch amongst a stack of legal briefs were Erin and Madison embracing in their briefs. Both of them vainly endeavored to cover up their semi-nude embarrassment.

Erin blurted out, "Jordan what a surprise."

"Yes it is, especially considering that this lovely woman here is your mother Erin. Forgive us for not calling first from the hospital where we located her, but we were in kind of a rush. Well I suppose everyone has a lot of catching up to do, so we'll be leaving." I retreated towards the front door shoving a smirking Travis in front of me.

Then Madison popped his head up. "Hi my name's Madison. Heard a lot about you Jordan."

Just then the police marched into Erin's living room and collared Travis and me. The cops announced, "Hold it right there. You two jokers aren't going anywhere."

"How'd these guys know we were jokers?" The cops ignored Travis.

Erin threw on her clothes and demanded, "Could you please tell me why you arresting these men officer?"

The arresting police sergeant explained, "These two clowns kidnapped this woman here from a mental hospital, and assaulted the head doctor."

Mrs. McNamara tried to explain, "These young men didn't kidnap me. I begged them to get me out of that horrible place. Besides, I was the one who punched Dr. Mengale' not them."

"Look we don't know who did what to whom, but the doctor is pressing charges so you two are coming down to the police station." The sergeant roughly cuffed Travis and me and started pushing us in the direction of the front door.

Erin nervously tried to adjust her unevenly buttoned blouse. "Officers this is my house. And, I am an attorney, and you don't appear to have a search warrant. In addition this woman is my mother and admitted in front of witnesses that she left the institution of her own volition. I don't think anybody wants a false arrest report filed tonight do they sergeant?"

The sergeant reasoned, "Look lady I can't show up at the station and tell this doctor that I let these two go just because you said so. They would probably lock me up. So if you want to come downtown and bail them out that will be fine." He then whisked Travis and me out the door, and drove us to the downtown Los Angeles lock up.

After arriving at the police station we were booked, and then thrown into a holding cell with some real criminals. One particular convict was so huge and hairy he made Travis and me look like women. Interestingly enough that's exactly what he wanted me to be. This hulking hillbilly inmate confided, "My name's Big Bubba, and you got some pretty lips on you boy."

I couldn't think of anything to say except, "Why thank you, thank you so much." However, the only thing going through my mind was that scene with Ned Beatty and those toothless crackers in "Deliverance".

I assumed that Big Bubba had seen the movie too. The big difference being that he thought "Deliverance" was a love story.

I have never smoked, but would have killed for a pack of cigarettes to bribe Big Bubba with. I whispered to Travis, "If Bubba grabs my ass and tells me to squeal like a pig just kill me."

Big Bubba began to shuffle menacingly toward me. He threatened, "You two boys talking about me? Big Bubba don't like it when people talk about him behind his back."

"We wouldn't dream of talking about you Big Bubba honest."

"You mean you don't like Big Bubba," he grumbled ominously?

Realizing that death or serious injury were our only options, Travis cautiously reached down in his sock. This made Big Bubba slowly back away. He must have thought it was a weapon.

Instead Travis produced a tightly rolled joint of marijuana and offered it to the retreating Bubba.

"Hear big guy a little taste of the chronic for you. Just stay over there all right?" Big Bubba nodded in agreement, and then he accepted and lit Travis's joint.

I reasoned, "Who would have ever thought that an illegal substance would actually save lives?"

"You shitting me? Getting high was the only way I could deal with working at that stupid mental hospital? It wasn't the patients. It was them damn doctors that was brutal."

We looked up from our conversation just in time to see a very stoned Bubba lumbering towards us with a crooked smile on his big ugly face. He mumbled, "Big Bubba needs sweets real bad. You boys got any cookies or candy on you?"

"Nice work Travis. Now you've created a Frankenstoner. What are we going to do now," I pleaded nervously?

Out of nowhere a guard arrived at the cell door. He yelled out, "Travis Wiley and Jordan Tyler let's get moving. You just made bail."

I have never been so relieved to see a uniformed officer in my entire life. Both Travis and I bolted out the cell door like a Laker fast break.

When we arrived at the front the desk sergeant stopped us. He asked Erin and Peggy, "Are these the two detainees you want released?" They nodded yes.

After Travis spotted the scowl on Peggy's face he was almost ready to go back in the cell with Big Bubba. I didn't have a clue what to say to Erin.

Sure I was still in love with her, but I couldn't get that picture of Erin with Madison on top of her out of my head. It wasn't exactly a Kodak moment, of course neither was the thought of Big Bubba. So I thanked both Peggy and Erin for bailing us out, but a policeman halted me. He asked, "Hold on there hot shot. We found a marijuana roach in your holding cell. You two boys know anything about that?"

Without even waiting for Travis to answer I looked the officer dead in the eye and lied, "No sir it doesn't belong to us. Must have been the big guy's."

The officer admitted, "We did strip search Big Bubba pretty carefully, but there is one particular area we didn't really want to check."

I thought to myself, well thank you for that mental picture Barney Fife.

Of course out loud I said, "Well I guess there's your answer right there. Can we be going now officer?"

The desk sergeant reluctantly handed both Travis and me two large envelopes. Then he instructed us, "Here is the stuff you came in with. Now don't let me ever see you two down here again. Got it?"

Travis and I nodded in compliance, grabbed our belongings, and beat Peggy and Erin to the exit. Before they arrived at the door Travis confessed, "With that look Peggy shot me I think I'd be better off taking the bus home."

"Are you sure? Remember Travis you are in downtown Los Angeles in the dead of night, and you're broke."

Just then Peggy and Erin caught up with us.

Peggy demanded, "Travis get in the car. I'm sure Erin and Jordan have a lot to talk about and I know we do." An ominous chill rented the air that had nothing to do with the weather.

I tried to explain, "Peggy it was all my fault. I talked Travis into breaking Erin's mother out the mental hospital."

"If you told Travis to jump off a roof, would he do that too? I don't think so. Well good night. We'll see you two later."

Ironically enough out of the two rides home, I would have chosen Peggy's. Even with that look on her face. Erin, however, could not have looked or smelled more alluringly. I, on the other hand, smelled like a downtown prison cell. Both of us entered her car in complete silence.

On the way home she divulged, "I'm really sorry about what happened Jordan. You and Travis put yourselves in a lot of jeopardy finding my mom for me.

I have been logging some long hours on Madison's divorce, as well as fending off his advances. Then the moment I gave in a little you all walked in."

"It didn't look like a little from where I was standing, then again Madison's big ass was blocking my view,"

Erin snapped, "Do you have to make a joke out of everything Jordan?"

"I'm sorry Erin. That's how comedians deal with pain, and I have been in a lot of it lately. Tonight did not help one damn bit."

"I'm sure it didn't. Please understand Jordan the last thing in the world I wanted to do was hurt you."

"Well evidentially it was on your list, because it really hurt."

Erin fumed, "If this is your way of showing me you love Jordan me, it is not what I want."

"Could women be any more confusing? I thought love was what you wanted. I've given you all of my love Erin. I even found your mother for you.

Is a ring and a damn piece of paper more important than that?"

"Perhaps it is. At this point I really need some solid security in my life Jordan."

"Security? Well then maybe you ought to marry Madison. If his wife doesn't take everything first."

Erin started to cry. "But I love you Jordan. I've always loved you."

"Did anybody ever point out you have a very strange way of showing it Erin?"

Erin dried her tears. "If that's how you feel, I'm just going to drive you straight home."

As Erin headed for my place I realize that I was letting the most incredible woman I'd ever met slip out of my life, but felt powerless to stop it. I tried to clarify my feelings. "I can't figure out what or who you want, and I'm not sure you know either Erin. All I know is that I feel very confused and wounded right now."

Over in Peggy's car the tone was a lot more explosive. She blistered Travis with, "What the heck were you thinking? I know Jordan talked you into this idiotic escape plan, that cost you the first real job you've had since I've known you; but did you have to go along with it?"

Travis responded sheepishly. "One of them doctors really chapped my hide Peggy, and besides Erin's mom wanted out of there."

"Freeing people from mental institutions was not in your job description," she pointed out.

"Yeah I know, but I did it for the right reason sugar babe."

"It doesn't matter. You both still owe me rent. Now you owe me bail money Travis."

In Erin's car things were not going any better.

She cryptically confirmed, "Perhaps you are right Jordan."

"About what?"

"About me marrying Madison. He did ask me you know."

At this point I didn't know if I should confess how much I loved her, or throw myself from her moving car. So I opened the car door.

"Hey what do you think you're doing? Close that door."

"No I want out of here right now."

"You are crazy. You know that, Jordan?" she shouted.

"Yeah I'm crazy in love, but you are too damn busy doing the horizontal hip hop with Ferrari-boy to care," I heatedly replied as I slammed the car door.

Erin pulled the car over to the side of the road. We looked directly at one another. She began to retaliate in anger, but instead we both hugged. Then she sighed deeply, let go of me, and we continued our drive in complete silence.

We all arrived at Peggy's condo at about the same time. Travis and Peggy exited her car, affectionately hugging and kissing, where there was a frosty detachment between Erin and myself. We looked at one another in complete bewilderment.

Erin mumbled a hasty good night and headed for her car. I ran after her, but all I caught were exhaust fumes. Peggy and Travis immediately noticed the stricken look on my face.

So Peggy put her arm around me and all of us went inside. Once upstairs she took me aside and asked, "What happened? How could you let her leave like that?"

"I don't know Peggy. We talked, we hugged; I guess we did everything except apologize. Look I'm just going to go to my room all right?" I got up, toddled to my room and closed the door behind me. After that I wondered why couldn't I have simply forgiven Erin and told her I would marry her?

Back at Erin's Madison had waited up for her. He opened the door the minute she arrived. She tearfully threw herself into Madison's arms. "Oh Madison this has been such a dreadful night. I'm afraid I am not going to be much company. I'm sorry. Perhaps you had better go home."

Madison wasn't sure exactly why Erin was crying. He attempted to comfort her by saying, "Are you certain? Sure this has been a pretty traumatic night. Seeing you mother after all these years. Don't worry. I put her to sleep in your back bedroom. She was exhausted."

Erin dried her tears. "Thank you Madison, but I really need to be alone right now."

Madison put his finger to her lips and said, "Shush. Let me at least tuck you in and make sure everything is all right."

In the meantime back at Peggy's, she had caught me on my way to the bathroom. "Pssst, Jordan? Come on tell me what happened between you and Erin? I know you want to talk about it."

"Not really, but you probably won't leave me alone until I do."

"That's right." Peggy smiled knowingly.

"Well, when we got in her car at the police station, Erin thanked me for finding her mother. Then she sort of apologized for being with Madison."

Peggy shot me a look of astonishment. "Let me get this straight. First she bails you out of jail, then thanks you for finding mom, and apologizes for her Madison fling? Just what were you waiting for, a declaration of love signed in her own blood?"

Right then I couldn't have felt more stupid. "I, I didn't know she was the one who had bailed me out. I assumed you did. I guess she did say she loved me, but I was way too caught up in my own anger to accept it."

Peggy was brutally honest with me. "Jordan for an bright guy your stupidity amazes me sometimes. All Erin wants is what all woman want. A man they can count on who will always be there for them."

"Come on, Peggy. Most of the time I can barely be there for myself." I sighed.

"Don't you realize that's probably why you found Erin in some one else's arms."

"Well then it is all about money isn't it?"

"If it were about money would I have married Travis?"

"I thought that just happened on a whim."

Peggy immediately changed the subject. "We were talking about you and Erin, remember? Now if I were in your shoes I'd go right over there and tell Erin exactly how much I love her, and that you were meant to be together for the rest of your lives."

"After catching her in the arms of some other guy? Wouldn't that be like rewarding bad behavior?"

Peggy shrugged and nodded yes. "Sure you're right, but being right doesn't always get you what you want does it? What you want is Erin. Now you have to convince her how serious you are about the relationship."

"By serious you mean offer to marry her, right?"

"It worked for Travis and me."

I reminded Peggy. "You of all people know I've already been down that lonely road and was left in a ditch for dead by my ex wife. Remember? Some poor guys have Viet Nam flashbacks. I still have flash backs about my first marriage."

Peggy stopped me cold with, "Please Jordan stop doing your act. It's about time you got over your silly little phobias. Don't you think? You should go over to Erin's house right now. I know you, and if you let this woman get away you will never ever forgive yourself."

"When you are right, you're right, Peggy."

"Women are always right, Jordan. Here: take my car in case yours won't start." She tossed me her car keys. I smiled a thank you back at her, and ran out the front door.

I left for Erin's with a head full of apprehensions, and a heart full of hope. As I pulled up in front of her house Madison was just leaving. If I was not mad before I certainly was now, but it was too late to turn back. As I got out of Peggy's car, Madison turned and kissed Erin good-bye. Then he drove off.

I walked right over to her and said, "I can't believe I came over to see if we could get back together and I catch you with Richy Rich again.

Damnit Erin! I don't know what to do. I love you so much it aches, but you just can't seem to keep your lips off that Armani wearing weasel."

"Will you be quiet long enough for me to explain what was really going on? Madison wanted to spend the night, but I told him he had to leave."

"Then what was that kiss all about?"

Erin paused then continued. "If you have to know, that kiss came after I told him that I didn't want to see him again. It was literally a good bye kiss."

"I really want to believe you Erin, because I have missed you more than life itself."

Erin hugged me tightly. "Why don't we go inside and you can show me exactly how much you missed me?"

As soon as she opened the front door Madison's Ferrari drove by. He slowed down and shouted, "See you tomorrow night kid." Then he raced off.

My face was livid with anger and betrayal. I growled, "Oh, I understand now. You didn't want to see him again until tomorrow night. I'll tell you what.

You can see him tonight if you want to, because I am out of here. Don't call, don't write, and don't e--mail. Good bye, Erin."

She tried to grab my sleeve as I stalked off in a huff. She yelled after me, "Stop, Jordan, and let me explain. He was just going to drop off more of his divorce papers. Please believe me."

I closed the car door on her last words and sped off into a night that was rapidly becoming morning. I'm glad I was driving Peggy's car or I may have been tempted to swerve into oncoming traffic. Just then a disc jockey on the car radio announced, "Hey, for all you LA lovers out there Happy Valentine's Day." I thought, *damn, there is irony everywhere, isn't there?*

When I arrived home, Peggy was just getting ready for work. She too one look at my forlorn carcass and surmised, "I guess things didn't go so well. You look awful."

"Well, thanks. That always makes me feel a lot better," I grumbled.

Peggy hugged me briefly. "I am sorry Jordan. Look I'm late for work as usual, so I've got to go. Bye."

She was out the door in a flash. So there I was I was all alone, with the Los Angeles sun rising on me and my misery. "Happy Valentine's Day Jordan," I muttered to myself as I slogged off to bed. My days slumber I had was fitful at best.

When I did finally wake up I noticed the sun was beginning to slip over the horizon. I stumbled into the kitchen and ran into Travis. The first thing out of his mouth was, "Man, you look like hell."

"People have been telling me that."

Travis tried to comfort me. "Peggy called and told me about you and Erin. That's a real bummer man. You gonna try to get her back, or do you want to go down to The Comedy Club tonight?"

"Are those my only two options?"

Travis thought for a moment. "Well I'm darn sure we're both out of a real job. So yeah."

"That reminds me: did you call the hospital to see if they have our checks ready yet?"

Travis stared at the floor before he answered. "They told me the doctor's busted nose would cost more than both of us made together."

"That's just great. It's just like our local comedy gigs. Again we work for free. I couldn't be more pleased."

Travis tried to cheer me up by suggesting, "Come on Jordan let's mosey down to the comedy club. Something good might turn up."

Before Peggy could return home we left for The Comedy Club in Travis's van. At this point both of us were running away from any actual employment and towards that vast abyss called Hollywood hope.

When we walked into Barry's club the other comics shunned us like we were lepers. I whispered to Travis, "Boy, what a difference a couple of days make. When these guys thought we could get them in our film project it was all buddy-buddy. Now we're being treated like registered sex offenders."

Travis instantly spotted the ex-studio executives Harvey and Bob.

They looked away when our eyes met theirs. "Jordan something is up and I don't think we're going to like it at all."

Just then the owner's son Matt climbed on the stage, and much to our amazement, he was very funny. Then Travis and I instantly realized why. It was because the little bastard was doing **my act.** At first Travis and I were too flabbergasted to speak. I tried to blurt out something, but the words stuck in my throat.

Then I realized why. It seems that the plagiarism of jokes and scripts in Hollywood is an all too common, salacious little local secret. It's kind of like an affable uncle who just happens to be a shameless pedophile. The question is do you drag the family through the disgrace of having a. favorite uncle committed, or lock him away in the basement with other dirty little family secrets?

Hollywood of course has opted for the family basement approach. This is the primary reason I felt powerless to do anything.

So I grabbed Travis and raced out the front door. He sputtered, "Do, do you believe that little son of a bitch is doing **your** act right in front of you? What the Hell are you going to do about it boy?"

"We could have his lips broken, but then we'd only land back in prison with Big Bubba. If I were still speaking to Erin we could get free legal advice. All right those are the two things we can't do." I shrugged out of frustration. "Why do I suddenly feel like an innocent bystanders at a drive by shooting?" Travis exploded, "Well we can't just do nothing. A lot of your act is in that darn script we wrote. Don't that protect us someway?"

I shook my head and answered, "I don't know. Did you get it registered or copyrighted?"

"I figured you did."

We looked at one another and simultaneously echoed, "We're screwed."

I thought for a second and then remembered. "I did mail a copy to Erin."

"Too bad you ain't on speaking to her."

At Erin's house she was pouring over legal documents when the doorbell startled her. She got up and cautiously checked through the peephole in the front door. On the other side was Madison grinning sheepishly. Erin yelled through the closed door, "Madison go home!"

"Please let me in. I have something very important to show you."

"Yeah I'll bet you do." She shouted back.

Erin's next-door neighbor opened his window and bellowed, "Let him show it to you already. Some of us are trying sleep over here."

Erin quickly opened the door and whispered, "Madison get in here. You'll wake up the whole neighborhood. What is so important that you had to come over at this hour?"

"Erin this is something that just couldn't wait." Then Madison pulled a small box out of his pocket and opened it. "I know you might consider this a little premature, but I'm asking you to be my wife. Here is my mother's antique engagement ring to make it official."

Erin stammered, "I, I don't know what to say Madison."

"Just say yes Erin. We were always meant to be together. You know it as well as do I." Before she could respond he slipped the ring on her finger. "See how gorgeous it looks on you. Now we are formally engaged. Keep that thought darling. I've got to relieve myself."

After Madison went to the bathroom Erin sat down on the couch. She lifted up a stack of legal papers. Under them was a manila envelope entitled "Script, rough draft". She opened it and started reading the pages inside. After only a few paragraphs Erin rolled over on her back and put it down. Tears began to well up in her big beautiful blue eyes. The two names at the bottom of the cover page were Jordan Tyler and Travis Wiley.

Erin picked up the script again and this time read aloud from them. "I have just been with the most incredible woman on planet earth. Her name is Erin McNamara. Basking in the light of her smile makes life seem worth living. She is the harmony of my heart, and hopefully shares my soul. Being with Erin makes the sunshine brighter and the moon even more mystical. If she could be mine I would live with her in eternal bliss. I have never nor will I ever love any one as completely as I do my Erin. I dedicate my life to her happiness. I'd tell her this in person, but it would probably end up with a punch line."

Erin cursed, pounded her fist on the bed, and exclaimed, "Damnit Jordan why couldn't you have told me this last night, before I got engaged to Madison?

Madison returned from the bathroom and asked, "What's wrong honey?"

Erin quickly buried the script under some legal briefs, and forced a smile. "Oh nothing."

Travis and I continued vociferously shouting at one another out in front of Barry's club. It was obvious how conflicted we were about what course of action to take.

Travis stung me with, "Jordan stop being a pussy. Get in there and tell that little bastard he's got no right doin' your act."

"Let me get this straight. First I toss Matt off of **his daddies stage.** This establishment happens to be LA's premier comedy club. Then and accuse him of stealing my material. Have I left anything out? Now for an encore I can get a giant spider web tattoo on my face and body pierce my ass. That will absolutely guarantee I'll never work in this town again."

"And if you don't go in there and stop that little turd right now, you won't be able do your act anywhere else either. He will own it."

I capitulated. "You're right. I have no choice. Once again I am screwed if I do and done for if I don't. Well let's go back in there and kick some serious comedy ass Travis. What do we have to loose except our careers?"

We marched back into the club just in time to hear Barry's kid on stage now bombing with my material. Comedy in the hands of an amateur can get down right ugly. I turned to Travis. "You know it's bad enough to steal my material, but to turn around and screw up my best jokes. Now that is un-fucking-forgivable."

At this point Barry's kid was flopping so badly that he was ripping off routines from Jerry Seinfeld to Rodney Dangerfield.

Barry shot me a don't you dare do anything look, and all I could did was smile and shrug my shoulders. Without another hesitation the MC and I leapt on stage at the same time. Matt reluctantly handed the microphone to the MC. The MC glanced at Barry and stubbornly relinquished the stage. "Well now we are going to be hearing some real comedy from the lips of Jordan Tyler. Give it up for him."

I smiled broadly at the scowling Barry, and began. "What a lovely crowd, and I do mean you sir. I used to be heterosexual until I got married. How many married people are out there?" A tepid burst of applause ensued. "A little hard to clap with those hand cuffs on isn't it kids. I know what you're thinking. What an a-hole, but he is right.

My ex even used to video tape our sex, so in court she'd have proof of mental cruelty. Yeah I had to pray for sex a lot. That's why they call it the missionary position. You have to hit your knees and beg for it. Ever had sex on one of those vibrating beds? I couldn't. I'd be too worried about the bed giving a better performance than me. I asked my ex if she ever fantasized about other men. She told me that I had dulled her senses beyond all imagination. She would complain I moved too slowly. I reminded her I was always quick in bed."

The audience loved the woman stuff so I pressed on. "Women love to tell you they have to be in the mood for sex. I notice they never have to be in the mood to shop. Dating can be brutal too. The one thing you never want to hear from a woman on the first date. There is something I forgot to tell you Jordan. It's about my penis. I am a comic so I had to ask if it were still attached, or was a snap on tool?"

I looked right in Barry's eyes and said, "Sex is tough enough, especially when you have a partner. Right Barry? Like you would know." The crowed roared. "When men are very y their brain calls a cab on them, because we are so blinded by our own sex drive. Then after sex men are even more sensitive. What's the first thing you hear ladies? **Snoring.** She'll say, 'I want to talk.' Men are out of it, ZZZZZZZZZ. Tell her, 'Just go shopping honey. I had to talk to get this far.' After sex the blood is not exactly in our brains. We would talk ladies, but the blood can only handle one large organ at a time."

The laughter swelled so I stayed on topic. "I found that a lot of married sex happens when you accidentally roll over on top of her in your sleep. Most of the time my ex wanted to cuddle instead of having sex. I've got a great idea too honey. Let's go to a jewelry store, and I'll let you wait outside in the car. Then I'll fly to romantic Maui alone, and leave you at the terminal being strip searched by a burly security guard."

I grinned. "Oh sure my marriage started off as a two way street, but it ended up as a toll road with limited access. Personally I would have had a lot more sex when I was married, but my wife would have just walked in and screwed it up anyway. My ex did have a sense of humor. Her vibrator and the knife sharpener made the same damn noise. So I didn't wear boxers or briefs. I wore low jack, because I want to know where my penis is at all times. Now that I'm single I shave one of my legs before I get in bed, so I can rub up against it. That way I can just make believe I'm with a another woman."

"Some men have Viet Nam flashbacks. I have flash backs about my ex wife. My marriage was a lot like a hurricane. First it blew and then it took my house. The best method of birth control for us was meeting with the parents before we had sex. Sure it was scary, but it worked. Remember boys and girls when you say I do, it could be the last time you agree on anything. I should get married again, because there is just not enough aggravation and violence in my every day life."

I was doing so well that Barry was waving me off the stage. So smiled innocently. "I'm kidding. I think they should do away with all TV violence, but only if they will replace it with full frontal nudity, starting with Richard Simmons. Yeah men are perverts. That's why I don't date them. They are just too rough and hairy. Answer me this. How can women pause in the middle of love-making and say, 'Stop it hurts?' We could suffer a groin pull and still have to finish."

"You try to be nice. After making love I'd ask my wife, "Did you have an orgasm honey?" She would tell me she got close, or I had a little one. What's up with that? It's pleasure ladies, let us in. If you had a really good one give me a high five. A chest bump would be nice. Take your diaphragm and spike it in the damn end zone, then do a little dance. I've spent at least a couple of minutes over here, let me know what's going on honey. Maybe that's why she had a twenty four second clock installed in our bedroom. The last time I saw my ex wife I asked her, did I come at a bad time? Her answer was that I **always** came at the wrong time. Thank you so much and good night."

A spontaneous burst of laughter and applause followed. I smiled at Barry, who was sitting with Harvey and Bob. They were even busting up and clapping. You know you have killed when even the people who are trying to screw you enjoy your act.

From the stage I paused to look out over the audience. Through the cheerful throng I observed a radiant Erin walking leisurely towards the stage.

I looked directly into her eyes. "I really want to thank you all a lot, because before I got on stage tonight I felt like my life was kind of empty. However, if this stunning woman here, Erin McNamara, will do me the honor of being my wife she would make me the happiest man in the universe. I have checked with the other planets."

When Erin walked up and kissed me the audience broke into spontaneous applause. Out of nowhere Madison appeared. Erin looked at me and I looked at Madison. He took out my hand and put a tiny box in it and said, "I think you're going to need this to make it official big guy."

I looked down at a ring that must have cost more than Madison's Ferrari. I was bewildered. "Thanks, but I don't get it. I thought we were rivals."

Madison confessed, "We were until I figured out that even if I did marry Erin she would never stop thinking about you. My ego could never handle that."

Erin and I both chuckled. She kissed Madison. I told him, "You're going to have to settle for a hand shake from me Madison."

Then I slipped the elegant ring on Erin's slender alabaster finger. I looked down at the ring and graciously said, "Madison I don't know how to ever thank you. This ring must have cost a fortune."

"Don't worry my ex wife would have just ended up with it anyway. I have always wanted Erin to have this ring."

Erin handed me my script and beamed. "I believe this is yours Jordan and now so am I." Erin hugged me so tightly I could hardly wait until we were alone together.

Barry rushed up to us and demanded, "Wait a damn minute. That script belongs to me now. Jordan and Travis forgot to have it registered."

Erin beamed triumphantly. "Perhaps so, but I didn't. Sorry Barry, this is a cease and desist order. If you continue to use this script in any form what so ever Jordan and I will own this nightclub."

She handed the crestfallen Barry some legal papers. He angrily ripped them up, and then moved menacingly towards me with a balled up fist.

Out of nowhere Erin's mother grabbed Barry's shoulder, spun him around, and drilled him right in the nose. The audience responded by giving her a standing ovation.

Barry's kid Matt whined, "But dad, what am I going to do for an act now?"

I advised. "It would be wise to find something more lucrative Matt, like living off your dad. And, Barry try to remember that comedy must always be used for good not evil."

Harvey and Bob came rushing over to me and pleaded. "Jordan we were always on your side, honest. We can still do this project. It's not too late."

"It is way too late for you guys, but it is just the right time for us."

I put my arms around Erin and her mom, and then we all exited the comedy club into a beautiful balmy Southern California night.

Right now I was aware that I had beaten the odds, and had found an honest love with a woman who meant more to me than any of my silly fears and phobias.

In fact I think all of us had discovered the thing that had been missing most in our lives. It was a sense of family. We were a strange little family to be sure; but then again, aren't most of them?

William Tyler Horn

Los Angeles

2000

www.ingramcontent.com/pod-product-compliance
Lightning Source LLC
Chambersburg PA
CBHW020613310726
48979CB00008B/1471/J

* 9 7 8 0 6 1 5 1 6 3 6 1 1 *